Back By Unpopular Demand

D.D. Richards

ISBN:0692687076
ISBN-13:9780692687079

DEDICATION

I dedicate this book to all the zero people who helped me write it and that non-existent person who inspired me to write it in the first place. And God...I guess.

CONTENTS

ACKNOWLEDGMENTS

Why Do They Always Assume You Want To Acknowledge Someone? I
Mean, How Often Do You Acknowledge Someone For Your Hard Work
Normally? I Pretty Much Never Do That. And I'm Awesome

DISCLAIMER:
Most of the stories you will read are 100% true if you ignore all reality and accept that life is a lie. Barring that, I would consider it safe if you believed about 87.43849% of what you read. Chances are that if something is just so ridiculous that there is no way an actual human experienced such an event that it is actually true and the more mundane stories are the ones made up. Thank George for those.

Note from the Author

What follows is a series of interviews conducted with an 18 year-old African-American college student at the end of his freshman year. Each chapter is "written" by one of his many displayed personalities and the person interviewed had final say on what went into the novel.

For example, once we had passed the 40,000 word count, he insisted we reach a total of exactly 50,000 words because, "It looks nice on the word document while you type." I tried to explain to him that the word count was inherently wrong because it included all the pointless information such as the table of contents, about the author, and dedication. He chose to ignore me. In all honesty, I regret my decision to do this. Writing this book was the worst decision in my life and I hated every moment I had to

My name is Jared. I'm your average depressed, socially anxious, sociopathic, orally fixated, paranoid, delusional, sadistic, microphilliac, hormonal, asexual, African-American, hypocritical, teenage, college student with insomnia, first-world problems, and multiple personalities. I used to think I had ADHD too, but then I realized that was just all the different voices in my head distracting me from doing certain tasks. Now I know what you're thinking, *"How in the world is this guy not in a mental institution?"* I blame the ignorance of others for my situation. Funny thing about having multiple personalities though: we don't all agree with one another.

Part of me takes full responsibilities for our actions. Part of me thinks it's all my mom's fault and part of me thinks it's my dad's fault. Part of me is certain we're ruled by an alien overlord and part of me is a devout Christian. One part of me became convinced that we live in a fictional story (hint: that's the part that inspired <u>Meta</u>). Which leads me into my next point. (Insert transition)

Future Maxwell Jones: Don't mind if I do.

Not-as-Future Maxwell Jones: Oh my goodness! They don't even know who we are yet.

Future Maxwell Jones: Well pardon me, but who has the most experience here.

Not-as-Future Maxwell Jones: That's not even fair. You're older by, like, ten minutes at most.

Future Maxwell Jones: Three days actually.

Growing up with multiple mental difficulties leads to problems that I'm pretty sure you can't imagine. The only way I can explain my probability-defying above-average functionality despite all my problems is through logic and complete guesswork. I think that the culmination of all the symptoms my problems caused eventually started cancelling different parts of each other out. Add that to my natural disposition of gullibility, creativity, and stubbornness along with some good fortune and you get a person who appears completely healthy despite having a broken mind. (Seriously, I should get paid to be studied by somebody famous).

Anyways let's get back on topic. And by "get back" I mean find one. I could write about movies, love, superpowers, truth, justice, liberty, America, Germany, war, peace, War and Peace, Warren Peace...um, words...tables...computers, letters (except that is kind of the same thing as words), animals. Oh! Animals! There we go.

Since I wrote this all out of order I realize now I have you at a disadvantage. All of us in here speak similarly but are quite different at a glance. Most of you won't want to read such apparent nonsense closely so Rayden came up with the brilliant solution of changing everybody's text when we type. It also kind of represents the differences in each of us. I'm sure this should help:

1. Jared
2. Reuben
3. Rayden
4. Simon
5. Maxwell Jones
6. George
7. Me
8. **Myself**
9. Damien
10. Daniel
11. *Nathan*
12. Casey
13. Samson
14. Nick
15. Harold

16. Thomas
17. Theodore
18. Steven
19. Kevin
20. Andrew
21. Ryan
22. Kyle
23. Jeremy
24. William
25. Malcolm
26. Richard
27. Jason

Chapter 1 Animals

I love insects. Especially ants. I could watch ants for hours. Come to think of it, I have watched ants for hours. Something about their seemingly mindless yet endless work ethic amazes me. Or I have a rare form of slight autism as well and slow repetitive behavior calms me. Which...wouldn't be that far-fetched.

But enough about me for right now. Let's talk about animals...and psychology. Did you know that we learned about mirror neurons by accident? Some researchers were doing...stuff to a monkey and had a whole bunch of... stuff hooked up to its brain. One day, a researcher (I think it was a lady) was eating ice cream as she walked past the monkey and the machine connected to its brain went off. It signaled that the monkey's brain was going through the same functions it would go through as if the monkey was eating, yet all the monkey was doing was watching the science lady eat. Boom! Scientific discovery.

Another fun fact: The same conditioning techniques people use to train pigeons, whales, and lions can be used to train people. It's called classical conditioning...or at least the easiest one is. I think it's amazing how humans can be so similar yet so different from all other animals at the same time.

In fact, a lot of stuff in psychology we learned from studying dogs. One recently cool thing an experiment found was that dogs, with good owners, had the reward centers of their brain go off when the owners returned after a long period of time (a few hours I think). The article I found that report in talked about how this proved dogs can feel love for humans. I disagree, but whatever.

What are with birds anyways? I mean, how do they stay

warm? They have no fur and the feathers don't seem to block much heat from escaping their bodies. A lot of species of birds migrate south for the winter which means that birds, in general, prefer warmer conditions. Maybe birds can't actually feel cold. Huh, I just thought about that. We can do as many tests as we want with current technology to tell ourselves all sorts of information about the animals around us, but we can never know how they actually *feel.*

Sure I can use an infrared camera to tell me when a bird's body is cold, but I can't read the bird's mind to tell me if the bird can actually feel cold. I know we can also hook up machines to their brains and see what kind of parts are activated in certain situations like with the monkey and dog examples previously, but all that tells us is what the brain perceives. There is too much evidence now for us to be ignorant and think the mind and brain are always on the same track. Heck, the most blatant evidence is staring at you right in the face as you read these words. Your brain interprets the electro-magnetic waves received from your eyes and turns them into electrical signals. Those signals form very specific patterns that you have trained your mind to recognize as letters. You also trained your mind to recognize what sounds certain letters make especially when placed in particular orders.

As you read your mind is doing all of that automatically at this point even when you get to words or letters that don't make any sense. Yqoue tyrnd to mksahe the words amake senince geecus thatsh what word ar supposed to d og. Your mind can also remember that certain combinations of letters have a meaning or implication that can be explained with even more words. And all of this happens so fast that you're not even consciously aware that you're doing it all of the time. In fact, try to listen to the voice that's reading you the words out in your head right now. Whose voice is it?

Whenever I write something down it's always my own voice that speaks the words that my fingers type. But when I read a book from someone else it depends. But I'll get to that in another chapter. Maybe. Probably not.

Previously I said I love watching ants, and I do, but my favorite insect is the praying mantis. I'm not exactly sure why either. Maybe it's how sleek and strange they look. Or how fast they can move. Or how deadly they are. I used to have a pet praying mantis and I would spend hours watching her just stand still in her cage. I fed her crickets and would wait for her to snatch one of them off of a branch so fast that if you blinked you would miss it. Man she was cool. (BTW, I know she was a she because she was pregnant and gave birth a few months after I got her)

Spiders are also cool even though they aren't insects. Spiders, bees, beetles, wasps, roaches, pill bugs, assassin bugs, flies, butterflies, water striders, and any others I can't think of right now are all amazing. And there are so many of each different kind. I don't get why people are so sad that Pokémon don't exist when almost every Pokémon is basically a recreation of something amazing that exists in the real world. We should be focused on training all the bugs and insects of this world to act like Pokémon.

Of course that won't happen anytime soon. Too many people hate so many of the Earth's most useful creatures. Flies, roaches, and beetles are basically living garbage dumps, compost bins, and fertilizers. The main point of most spiders is to keep the population of dirtier creatures under control. They're kind of like cops that way (especially considering how many people hate them for doing their job). I have a personal vendetta against bees and wasps, but I can't ignore that they pollinate and maintain a wide variety of plants that produce, quite literally, life-giving oxygen.

Pretty much every negative you can find for every insect or bug has a positive that matters more. Probably why we don't force them into extinction.

Except mosquitos. Mosquitos are actually useless. You may say, *"But mosquitos kill the most humans every year. Without them the world would overpopulate much faster!"* Got some bad news for you. The world is going to overpopulate no matter what; unless murder finally becomes encouraged. Plus, if the only positive attribute of something that you can come up with is that it kills a lot of people every year you might want to redefine your definition of positive.

I'm not the only one to realize how useless mosquitos are either (and, no, I don't count the other voices in my head as other people...this time). Scientists once ran a test where they put 100 bats in an enclosed environment where their only food source were mosquitos. You know what happened after a reasonable period of time? The mosquito population had increased. Not only does the mosquito make up less than 1% of a bat's diet, but even when mosquitos are literally the only thing to eat bats still can't keep their population under control.

Honestly, the only good thing mosquitos do is kill humans considering how much of a detriment we are to the planet. If we imagine Earth as a living organism (which it pretty much is) then mosquitos are the antibodies trying to rid the Earth of the virus called humanity. Maybe that's why we can't kill all of the mosquitos; the Earth actually makes them like we make white blood cells.

Speaking of tiny things swimming around in our bodies, did you know viruses and bacteria are technically animals? It's amazing how certain things can be all classified together in science yet so separated in culture. Like how we teach young kids that fish live underwater and mammals live on land but then have to make the distinction that some mammals live underwater yet some fish don't live on land. Then some things that live underwater aren't fish at all, but they also aren't reptiles or amphibians. And some amphibians live underwater for part of their life and then on land for the rest. Birds are the creatures who can fly...except for some of them who behave similarly to reptiles or mammals. All mammals give live births except for the few that don't and the one species of lizard that does. Humans are the most advanced and dominant animal on the planet, but are physically weaker than several other animals and have lower IQs than dolphins (I never did get how they even tested that). Ants, bees, and other insects have a better work ethic than humans. Humans can't see in the dark very well. And share over 90% of their DNA with chickens.

You know, when I start listing all the stupid things that go on in the world it starts to sound a little depressing. Heh heh heh heh heh heh heh heh heh heh heh heh heh heh heh.

List #1 Movie Mistakes

SO I KNOW I ALREADY DID A LIST SIMILAR TO THIS IN MY FIRST BOOK, SO I'VE TOOK SOME TIME OUT TO THINK OF A WAY TO MAKE IT NEW AND INVENTIVE. SO I ASKED MY FRIENDS TO GIVE ME A LIST OF MOVIES FOR ME TO CRITIQUE AND RANT ABOUT. I ASKED THEM TO GIVE ME ANY MOVIE FOR ME TO FIND THE MISTAKES EVEN IF THE MOVIES CONSIDERED TO BE AMAZING OR NEAR PERFECTION.

A COUPLE THINGS BEFORE WE BEGIN. FIRST, I HATE VERY FEW MOVIES. SECOND, I DID WATCH EACH OF THE MOVIES MENTIONED AFTERWARDS AT LEAST ONCE. THIRD, HA.

HERE WE GO! (IF YOU DIDN'T SAY THAT IN MARIO'S VOICE THEN I'M SORRY YOU CAN'T FEEL JOY ANYMORE. GO EAT SOME CHOCOLATE.)

SPEAKING OF CHOCOLATE, DO YOU KNOW WHY LIFE IS LIKE A BOX OF CHOCOLATES? BECAUSE THE ONLY WAY SOMETHING BROWN MAKES IT IN AMERICA IS IF IT'S RICH AND SERVES A PURPOSE DETERMINED BY WHITE PEOPLE TO BE GOOD OF COURSE! NOW, I CAN IGNORE THE BLATANT SYMBOLISM BETWEEN FORREST AND AN AFRICAN-AMERICAN EVEN THOUGH HIS BELOW AVERAGE INTELLIGENCE, SEXUAL PROWESS, GREAT ATHLETIC ABILITY, AND SOCIAL OUTCAST NATURE IS QUITE HARD TO IGNORE. I CAN EVEN IGNORE JENNY'S DIABOLICAL MANIPULATION OF A POOR AND ALMOST RETARDED MAN INTO AN ABUSIVE RELATIONSHIP. I MEAN, "I LOVE YOU FORREST AND WANT YOUR HELP BUT DON'T HELP ME BECAUSE I LOVE YOU AND YOU LOVE ME AND YOU SEE ME IN DANGER EXCEPT FOR WHEN I THANK YOU FOR SAVING ME WHEN I'M IN DANGER BECAUSE I STILL LOVE YOU. PLUS, NOW YOU

HAVE A KID AND PROBABLY AIDS BECAUSE IT'S THE SEVENTIES AND I WAS A HIPPIE FOR A FEW YEARS." I MEAN, IT'S STILL A BETTER LOVE STORY THAN TWILIGHT...BUT ONLY BARELY.

WHAT I CAN'T FORGIVE IS PROBABLY THE BIGGEST PLOT HOLE IN THE ENTIRE MOVIE. FORREST IS A HOMETOWN HERO, COLLEGE FOOTBALL STAR, WAR HERO WHO MET TWO PRESIDENTS OF THE UNITED STATES, DR. PEPPER ENTHUSIAST, OLYMPIC PING-PONG CHAMPION, ONE OF THE ORIGINAL APPLE INVESTORS, AND THE COFOUNDER OF THE BIGGEST SHRIMPING COMPANY IN AMERICA YET NOT A SINGLE PERSON AT THAT BUS STOP KNEW WHO HE WAS. ONE OF THE MEN EVEN RECOGNIZED THE SHEER DESCRIPTION OF THE FAMOUS SHRIMPING COMPANY, BUT COULDN'T EVEN FATHOM THAT FORREST WAS THE OWNER OF THE COMPANY EVEN THOUGH HIS PHOTO WAS IN MULTIPLE PAPERS AND MAGAZINES WHEN THEY BECAME FAMOUS!

OUR NEXT MOVIE IS NO SAINT, BUT IT DOES HOLD A SPECIAL PLACE IN PEOPLE'S HEARTS AS ONE OF THE BEST HORRIBLE MOVIES EVER MADE. I MEAN, "YOU'RE TEARING MEE? APART LIZSSA! YOU'R ARE TARING MEHY APART!" IS ONLY ONE OF THE MANY MEMORABLE LINES AND MOMENTS FROM THIS TRAVESTY. WHY DO THEY PLAY FOOTBALL SO MUCH? THEY DON'T EVEN PLAY FOOTBALL! THEY JUST THROW A BALL BACK AND FORTH WITHIN ABOUT TEN FEET OF EACH OTHER AS IF THEY FEEL A NEED TO FILL UP TIME BETWEEN ONE OF FIVE DIFFERENT SCENES BEING SHOWN. SERIOUSLY, EACH SCENE IS EITHER JOHNNY'S BEST FRIEND FEELING CONFUSED AND/OR CONFLICTED ABOUT CHEATING WITH LISA, LISA'S MOM TELLING LISA JOHNNY IS A GOOD MAN, JOHNNY DOING SOMETHING STUPID AND JUST NOT HUMAN, COMPLETE RANDOMNESS THAT GIVES NO WEIGHT TO THE PLOT OR REALLY ANYTHING ELSE IN ANYBODY'S LIVES, OR YOU SLEEPING BECAUSE NOTHING

HAPPENS IN THE MOVIE!

I LOVE THE ART OF THE BAD MOVIE AND THIS ONE IS A REAL STINKER, BUT IT CAN'T REALLY BE THE BEST OF THE WORST OF THE WORST BECAUSE NOTHING HAPPENS. IT'S FUNNY TO LAUGH ABOUT HOW STUPID ALL THE CHARACTERS ACT, BUT IF YOU REALLY THINK ABOUT IT WHAT MATTERED? WHAT WAS THE STORY? THERE'S A GUY WHO IS IN A FAILING RELATIONSHIP WHO LOSES HIS JOB AND COMMITS SUICIDE? WHY? WHY DID THAT STORY NEED TO EXIST? I KNOW WHAT YOU'RE THINKING, "WELL, WHY DOES ANY FICTIONAL STORY EXIST?" EASY, THEY EXIST BECAUSE WE EITHER WANT THEM TO OR NEED THEM TO. HARRY POTTER EXISTS BECAUSE WE LOVE TO WATCH AN ABUSED CHILD RISE UP AGAINST A TYRANNICAL AND EVIL OVERLORD THROUGH HIS COURAGE AND HELP FROM HIS FRIENDS OVER THE COURSE OF HIS ENTIRE LIFE. HIS STORY MATTERS BECAUSE WE ARE INVESTED IN IT. EVEN BAD STORIES LIKE PRETTY MUCH EVERY SURVIVAL FICTIONAL (I.E. CAST AWAY) MAKES YOU FEEL THE DANGER THE CHARACTER OR CHARACTERS FEEL. I THINK IT'S A BAD FORM OF STORYTELLING, BUT IT IS STILL TELLING A STORY.

IT MATTERS THAT HE GETS THAT TOOTH OUT, SO WHEN YOU SEE HIM SLEEP ON THE FLOOR OF THE HOTEL ROOM YOU FEEL SOMETHING ALONGSIDE THE FICTIONAL CHARACTER. THAT DOESN'T HAPPEN IN THE ROOM. THEY AREN'T STEREOTYPES OR INSENSITIVE PEOPLE. THE CHARACTERS AREN'T SO OVERDRAMATIC TO BE ENTERTAINING. AND THE STORY DOESN'T EVEN EXIST BEYOND AN, THOUGH I HATE TO ADMIT IT, INTERESTING PREMISE. I SUGGEST THAT THE NEXT TIME YOU WATCH THIS MOVIE YOU AND YOUR FRIENDS MAKE SOME SORT OF DRINKING GAME OVER HOW OFTEN "PLOT" ELEMENTS ARE COPY AND PASTED DURING THE RUNTIME.

ACTUALLY, DON'T DO THAT BECAUSE YOU'LL LIKELY DIE FROM ALCOHOL POISONING.

SPEAKING OF MOVIES WITH PLOT PROBLEMS...AVATAR. THE ONE BY JAMES CAMERON. I'M NOT EVEN SURE WHERE TO START WITH THIS ONE. EVERY CRITIC ON YOUTUBE HAS POINTED OUT HOW THE PLOT BASICALLY RIPS OFF EVERY "SAVE THE TREES" MOVIE OR NATIVE AMERICAN MOVIE IN EXISTENCE. SO I WANT TO FOCUS MORE ON THE ELEMENTS THAT ARE UNIQUE TO AVATAR...OR, AT LEAST, AS UNIQUE AS YOU CAN GET NOWADAYS.

FIRST, OUR PROTAGONIST. WHAT WAS HIS MOTIVATION AGAIN? OH YEAH, HE WAS A **SOLDIER** WHO WAS **ASSIGNED** THE TASK OF PROTECTING **HUMAN** SCIENTISTS ON AN ALIEN PLANET. THEN THE GENERAL GIVES HIM A NEW DIRECTIVE TO **INFILTRATE AND ANALYZE** THE DEFENSES OF THE NATIVE PANDORIANS SO THE **HUMAN** MILITARY WILL HAVE AN ADVANTAGE IN **WIPING THE SPECIES OUT FOR PROFIT.** AND THE ONLY REASON JAKE WAS EVEN THERE WAS BECAUSE HE SHARED THE GENETIC CODE OF HIS TWIN BROTHER WHO WAS ORIGINALLY SUPPOSED TO BE A PART OF THE RESEARCH TEAM. JAKE GIVES UP ON ALL OF HIS ORDERS AND DUTIES AS BOTH A SOLDIER AND A HUMAN BECAUSE HE ASSIMILATES TO THE NA'VI CULTURE. I MEAN, WHY?

SECOND, THE EFFECTS. I REALIZE THAT THE MAIN (ONLY) REASON THIS MOVIE BECAME FAMOUS AND MADE SO MUCH MONEY WAS THE INCREDIBLE EFFECTS. AND I WON'T DENY THAT THEY LOOK FANTASTIC...ON A BIG SCREEN. THEY LOOK ABOUT AS AMAZING AS CURRENT VIDEO GAMES AS SOON AS YOU SCALE THEM DOWN FROM A MOVIE SCREEN TO A TELEVISION SCREEN. IF AN EFFECT ONLY LOOKS GOOD IN LARGE

SCALE, THEN IT'S NOT A GOOD EFFECT. PLUS, ALL OF THE DESIGNS OF THIS "ALIEN" WORLD ARE BORING. OKAY, THOSE DRAGON THINGS WERE PRETTY COOL, BUT EVERYTHING ELSE CAN BE DESCRIBED AS A (INSERT NOUN) FROM EARTH BUT BIGGER, MAYBE A DIFFERENT COLOR, AND WITH EXTRA LIMBS.

THE NAVI? BIG BLUE PEOPLE WITH TAILS. THE HORSES? LITERALLY JUST BIGGER HORSES WITH SIX LEGS. EVEN THE SUPPOSED SPIRITUAL PLANT SPERM LOOKING THINGS ARE JUST POLLEN SPORES THAT ARE MAGICAL BECAUSE THE MUSIC TELLS YOU THEY ARE AND THE CHARACTERS LOOK AT THEM WITH AWE. WHAT'S THE POINT OF RETELLING THE SAME STORY AS FERNGULLY, BUT WITH ALIENS, WHEN YOU DO NOTHING TO MAKE THE ALIEN WORLD DIFFERENT FROM EARTH?

ACTUALLY, MAKING IT AN ALIEN PLANET IS WORSE FOR THE STORY YOU'RE TRYING TO TELL. IF THE MESSAGE IS "SAVE THE TREES" OR "BIG COMPANY BAD, NATURE GOOD" THEN WHY MAKE HUMANS THE BAD GUYS? I CERTAINLY DON'T CARE IF WE RUIN THE ECOSYSTEM OF AN ALIEN PLANET IF IT MEANS HUMANITY BENEFITS AS A WHOLE. THE PROBLEM WITH ASSAULTING AND "CIVILIZING" THE NATIVE AMERICAN PEOPLE LONG AGO WAS IT WAS HUMANS VERSUS MORE HUMANS. THERE SHOULDN'T HAVE BEEN ANY CONFLICT BETWEEN TWO CULTURES OF THE SAME SPECIES. BUT IN AVATAR, IT'S THE HUMAN RACE VERSUS A LARGE AND INTIMIDATING ALIEN RACE WITH STRANGE ABILITIES AND "MAGICAL" POWERS. UGH, THIS MOVIE AND ITS PROBLEMS ARE TOO WELL-KNOWN. LET'S MOVE ON.

Chapter 3 Sitting Outside Ashley's Room

Why am I here right now? I don't know. Maybe I'm lonely. I mean, I knew this was coming. Everyone would go away for Spring Break and I would be here. Alone. It's not like I ever needed people before...I mean, this was the whole reason I got rid of such desires in the first place. Guess if they're back I didn't really get rid of them.

And then there's ___. I think she's a nice girl. Honestly, I don't know what attracted me to her in the first place. Just one of those things again. Oh good, the fight scene. Ashley's in there watching a movie about dead people. I thought we were going to watch it together, but I guess I made her mad or something. People are like that. Rather watch a movie alone because a friend did something strange.

Why am I being punished for being myself? That's what it always feels like. I never seem to be rewarded for my behavior unless I'm doing what everybody else wants me to do. Yet people tell me that my behavior is a self-fulfilling prophecy of some kind. That I intentionally drive people away because I expect them to be driven away. Which could be true, but I don't like that. It doesn't fit my character traits.

I am the character that breaks the fourth wall. I do it all the time when I talk to the author of this story we live in.

Let's see just how good I've gotten so far.

She sits across from me, a little to the right actually. I've lent her my pillow since we're sitting on the floor. She tells me about her own novel. A group of kids trying to get into a weird college with a strange application process. "Not realistic, but they are humans, not flying unicorns." Her brown hair shines in the pale light. The plainness of her face is exuberant.

More dialogue about a literary magazine at our college. She fiddles with her phone and her lanyard as she talks about her hopes, her desires. Is she nervous? Idle? Bored? As I type across from her do I bore her? Red shoes, blue jeans, and a gray top. Chapped lips, yet I find it okay. She isn't about looks, but the pure energy coming from her voice and her movements.

The departed plays in the background against the harsh typing of my fingers against the keys. The half-smile permanently fixed to her face. A black watch hangs off her right arm. A more relaxed pose emerges. A snapchat. A sorority. "Conforming to social norms. I guess."

Grey socks. Is this the right thing to do? Focus on the physical? While she talks. "It would be nice to delete everything." An annoying voice to fit an annoying story. A believer of organized chaos. And she's gone. Not bad if I say so myself.

Alone again, here I sit. Outside waiting for adventure. Ashley's still in the room. The movie still plays. Maybe she fell asleep. Maybe she can't hear me. She must

be able to hear me. The walls are thin and my voice is loud.
Maybe I should leave. Go back to my room, watch some
YouTube, drift off to sleep to the sound of pleasant music.
The talk with ___ went well enough. It was interesting.

Chapter 4 Now You Get It

The joke that is. You get it now. Unless now was before then this doesn't make any sense at all and I'm just confusing you. Doesn't matter.

Let me introduce myself. My name is Maxwell Jones and I am a master of time and space. And not like phony masters you would see in a movie or television program, but an actual master that can manipulate time and space to my will. There are limitations because time and space are restricted in their own properties, but I'm sure you already know that now. Or at least you will know it now because I told you earlier.

There is one drawback to being a master of time and space. In order for you to understand fully I need to take you back a few years to when I first realized time was something that could be controlled.

I was in fifth grade when I decided to read a biography of Thomas Jefferson. It described a moment in his life when he was sitting through a boring class and desperately wanted to leave in order to do something more worth his time (at least worth his time from his perspective). He discovered, that day, that if he put all of his attention into a task instead of splitting his attention between a task and watching time go by that time seemed to move faster.

Most of us realize or have heard of this phenomenon before, so I did not take note of it. I did use the technique to get through several boring and tedious points in my life, but it wasn't until high school that I realized the implications of time's relative nature.

Each of us have our own timeline that contains all possibilities that we can and will go through during our existence. A lot of our timelines cross and depend on one another. For example, if your father doesn't go to a certain café at a certain point in his timeline he won't get a cup of coffee with a particular blend. If he doesn't get that particular blend of the coffee, what he does get will not put him at the correct level of alertness to notice a beautiful young woman walk past him on his way to work. If he does not see that woman he does not fall in love with her, marry her, or make you with her. Thus the beginning of your timeline begins (or in that case, doesn't begin) before you ever do.

Not only do we each have our own timeline, but each of us travels along it at the same average rate. Some of us move faster than others at random points in time, but then move slower than others at other points in time to balance it out. In fact, there is not a way to truly cheat the amount of time you are allotted without doing as I have done. And even that is risky as I explained earlier.

As my interest peaked about time's relativity I began to notice a fundamental problem in exploring the limits of time: I was bounded within time. Everything we study in science comes from being outside of the studied environment. If we study a plant, we cut apart and look into the plant. If we want to study humanity, we look at certain groups of humans that can represent the average person. However, we cannot truly study time because we are always within its effects. It is like trying to diagnose yourself with a disease. The effects of the disease have an effect on your own behavior thus you cannot trust your own diagnosis.

So I decided to remove myself from time in order to learn everything I could about time. I searched for a way to do so for about a year before I found the answer during a dream. I found another dimension. I mentioned it before in my first book, but I want to go into more detail about what the Nth Dimension is and how I study it. First of all, I have no physical proof that the Nth Dimension exists outside of what I've experienced. Funny thing is I don't see a need for proof to myself since I've actually experienced it.

First of all, time is not a real factor inside consciousness. Sure you can still perceive it as existing but its relevance to the goings on of your mind is fairly insignificant. Similar to the example about making a tedious task go by quickly by focusing your mind, focusing your mind allows you to manipulate your timeline. Unfortunately, I have not found a way to break free from my social conditioning to stay in the Nth Dimension for longer than thirty minutes at a time.

At first, I could only go into the ND (my abbreviation) for a few seconds or maybe a minute in "real" time but it felt like I spent hours creating or looking around in the ND. We would normally call this phenomenon daydreaming, which it is. But haven't you ever wondered why dreams are so mysterious to us?

Think about the decades of research conducted on dreams yet we still can't determine exactly why we dream. My theory is simple: humans are meant to live in the ND (outside of time) but for some unknown reason we are bounded in the wrong dimension. Our only escape is through dreaming which is why an absence of dreams, for a long period of time, drives people crazy.

Second of all, the ND has interesting properties dealing with energy and humanity. While inside the ND I "see" everything even though everything is black. I can see different waves and particles flowing through the world and through different people. It took a few weeks of practice but I was eventually able to leave the physical bounds of my own consciousness and go into other people's minds. I know that sounds crazy, but I don't have an excuse so deal with it.

The first time I did this it hurt...a lot. I had a headache for about an hour. After practicing every few hours every day, the pain faded into nonexistence and I was able to freely explore through the non-physical world simply by focusing my mind and letting myself go into the ND. And this is where it gets interesting.

Future Maxwell Jones: I can't believe I thought this would be a good idea.

Present Maxwell Jones: Not again.

Future Maxwell Jones: I mean, nobody cares about the actual science of time travel and relativity. All they hear is a crazy person spouting nonsense.

Present Maxwell Jones: Why do you always do this? Every time I talk about something cool or inventive all you do is talk about how horrible I am.

Future Maxwell Jones: You are horrible. I mean, "The first time I did this it hurt...a lot." That's not even good writing let alone scientific or informative exposition.

Present MJ: First of all, I am you.

Future MJ: More like a shadow of me.

Present MJ: Fine then, what should I be talking about?

Future MJ: Definitely not time travel. Talk about temporal relevance or our theory of gravitational waves.

Even more Future Maxwell Jones: (By the way, this part was written before gravitational waves were actually confirmed in the scientific community and it was an actually theory of mine. I imagined gravitational waves as high frequency and unstable amplitude waves.)

Present MJ: I don't think our target audience is ready for our more theoretical ideas quite yet.

Future MJ: But they are ready for an entirely new dimension where they can travel through time and space at will.

Present MJ: Well, yes. But—

Future MJ: And in this dimension they can see energy as a particle the same way we observe electrons and protons.

Present MJ: I get it.

Future MJ: And not only is this a serious theory, of which you have no solid proof or anything closely related to evidence, but you actually expect people to give you money to research it.

Present MJ: I hadn't even gotten to that part yet.

Future MJ: I know. I made sure to interrupt before you wasted our time with all your nonsense.

Present MJ: Well mission successful. I will no longer discuss time and the Nth Dimension.

Future MJ: Good.

Maybe I'm right and I shouldn't be playing around with time this much. All this inconsistency and paradox could drive a person insane.

Chapter 5 Lies That Bind

When I was a wee lad, my cousins from the country and I would wrestle and fight. I was pretty tiny, and the youngest, so most people would expect me to lose. But they underestimated my lack of understanding as to what "play-fighting" was. So I bit my cousins and won. They grew scared of me after being bitten and choked several times and we stopped fighting with each other.

When I was in the fifth grade, I raced my mom's van up one of the many hills in our neighborhood. I won. Nobody believes me, but I was there. I know what happened. It was a close race too.

During my elementary career, my dad and I would wrestle in the living room all the time. He only beat me a few times. Once, I was stuck underneath him, but knew I had to win, so I strained all of my muscles and lifted him into the air for a split second in order to escape.

I didn't do anything special to train the physical perfection that was my body. I played outside pretty much every day since I didn't have video games and only watched a few educational TV shows after finishing my homework. I rode my bike, ran at the park, practiced my swing set technique, played soccer, took karate for a year, played basketball, tee-ball, baseball, golf, took multiple swimming lessons (I was a natural at the dolphin technique), and was chosen as the second fastest kid in my class in fifth grade. Well, the teacher told me, in private, that I was actually the fastest which is why he put me in a spot that slower runners would lose pace at.

I was in seventh grade when I saw a kid getting picked on by this asshole named Dillon (or Dylan, I don't care how he spells it). I ran over to protect the kid being bullied because I had past experience at the school to let me know that adults were useless at that sort of thing. I pulled the kid out of Dylan's hands and punched him in the stomach to get him to back off. And he laughed. "What was that?" He chuckled at me. I pushed him away and walked off with the kid he was bullying. Dylan and his posse walked off as well, now bored with their victim, still laughing at my attempt to hurt him.

I went home, still pondering what had happened, and decided to do a test. I went up to my dad and punched him in the stomach and he doubled over in pain. But this time I saw the truth. Those small hints of a smile on his face. The proud yet bored look in his eyes. The way his body was relaxed instead of tense. He was faking pain. And I had fallen for it.

I felt like such a fool as I thought back to all my precious feats of physical prowess and saw them for what they really were. I wasn't a great swimmer; I was an eleven-year-old in a class with seven-year-olds. I wasn't a soccer champion; I only played a few games in the season and everybody in the league got a trophy. I didn't hit a homerun; the other team let me score. I didn't outrun a speeding car uphill; my mom had intentionally gone slow enough for me to beat her. I wasn't one of the fastest or strongest kids in the grade; I was the tiny little nerdy kid everybody was nice to so I would help them with school.

Everything was a lie.

So I decided to change everything the only way we can in this cruel world. I got stronger. Every morning I woke up thirty minutes earlier and went into the bathroom to get ready for school. I did twenty push-ups, fifty calf raises, and twenty sit-ups before leaving the bathroom. I walked as fast as I could from class to class during the school day. I took stairs two at a time, jumping on one leg, or by using only my arms and the handrails to up and down the stairs. After school, I would go to the track and run three miles.

After about a year and a half I was doing one hundred pushups without stopping, forty sit-ups with a twist at the top, one hundred calf raises, eight miles, could jump up six stairs at a time from rest, and it felt amazing. Veins were popping out of my arms and legs, my calves were toned and defined. You could see the individual muscles in my quads. I even started working out my fingers to build strength and flexibility.

In the summer of eighth grade, my dad signed me up for a summer workout program my school had for two weeks. We were weightlifting 3 days in the week and doing conditioning the other two days. To my surprise, I was much stronger than the other kids my age. I loved it.

I signed up for the weight training class my school offered in high school as a PE credit every semester. Something about throwing large amounts of weight around made me feel better about myself. And nobody could deceive me of my feats when the amount of weight was printed in large numbers on everything. I drank protein shakes and went to extra workout times after school to get as big and as strong as possible.

I'll admit I wasn't completely motivated just by the lies I was told as a child. I also did it because I was a fairly short person and the only control I had over my growth was how much space my muscles could take up.

I began teaching myself how to fight. I found a retired boxer to train me during the summer. I continued fencing and tried to form new techniques that could be translated into real-world combat skills. I asked one of my coaches to keep giving me new physical challenges to overcome every few weeks so I wouldn't grow docile. When I saw somebody lifting fifty pounds in the weight room I would walk over, add another twenty pounds, and lift it three times as fast as they could.

I despise weakness. I despise deception. Which is why I do not lie about how weak we are as individuals. How weak we allow ourselves to be. When I'm lying down on the bench or standing underneath the squat bar I don't do a single rep unless I know I can't lift more than what I put on the bar. Once, I was doing an exercise incorrectly because the weight I was using was so light that I didn't need to move my body in the correct way to move the weight around. I never made that mistake again.

I drew pleasure from failing to lift a weight because that meant I had a new goal to overcome. I began doing hundreds of jumps with eighty pounds added to me. I broke the bench, squat, and pull-up record for my weight class at my school. I never could get close to the vertical jump record because of my height. Something about gravitational restraints on how high I can jump due to my muscle mass and height. I'll find a way around it soon.

As I grew older I noticed a skill I had to identify the weaknesses in others and how to fix them. After learning the ropes in my first two years of Performance Training, the weight lifting class, I only took freshmen on as my partners. They needed an informed trainer to build their potential. And it showed. Under my guidance, each of my partner's maxes went up forty pounds a semester. My last partner, Peter, went from barely being able to bench the bar to benching a 35 lbs. weight on either side in one year.

Sadly, I can't be there for everybody all the time. They need to learn how to do what I did for myself in seventh grade. You need to learn how to be strong. You need to learn how to be tough. And here's how.

First of all, some disclaimers. Not everybody is the same. Not everybody can just start a workout regimen for themselves the way I did. Not everybody progresses at the same rate. That's why the first challenge is one of the most important and one of the hardest.

Challenge 1: Test your limits. All of them. How long can you function without eating? Without sleeping? (Never try without water. Water is your best friend and you should always have at least a half-gallon by your side at all times from now on). How long can you stand on the hot pavement without shoes? How fast can you run a mile? How many pushups can you do without slowing down? Without stopping? How many punches can you do in ten seconds with one arm?

Don't try to find out all of your limits within a few days. You'll hurt yourself. The key to fulfilling this challenge is to never stop with it. Always look for new opportunities to test yourself. To push yourself to become stronger. Maybe you're walking to a class outside and it starts raining. Instead of immediately covering up to avoid getting wet, see what happens to you when you let the rain soak through to your bones. Wear sandals instead of boots the next time it snows. Stare directly into the sun when it shines in your eyes. Don't take any medicine or stop your daily routine when you catch the flu.

Your body can withstand more than you give it credit for. It can do so much more than you allow it to. The way I think about it is this: When a really fat and out-of-shape person walks for a long time they get tired. Yet the average person can walk for almost forever because walking is something they do all the time. People on athletic teams (who are actual athletes, not golfers) tend to be able to jog at their own pace for as long as they want because their bodies are used to higher levels of activity. Imagine what would happen if you jogged everywhere you went for the next ten years. Jogging would become like walking is for you now and running would be like jogging.

The same logic applies to your other abilities. The more you expose yourself to extreme temperatures the more you will feel comfortable in them. The more damage your body heals and recovers from the more damage you will be able to resist in the future.

So test your limits. Break through them. Don't be afraid of the pain that will come. Know that your body will recover from it. It will take time, and a lot of effort, but it will be worth it.

Challenge 2: Train your muscles. A strong body is a healthy body. Every part of your body can become stronger. And the strength I'm talking about isn't the stuff Arnold Schwarzenegger or Hulk Hogan had. I'm talking about Muhammed Ali strength. You see, there are two types of ways to build muscle: one is to rip your muscles apart and then supplement them with protein, carbs, and fat so that they grow bigger and longer as they recover. Two, is to make the muscles on your body tougher, denser, more resistant to fatigue.

Weightlifting will build the first kind, but bodyweight exercise will build the second kind and the second kind is more valuable. What is the point in being as strong as an ox if you can only lift something really heavy three times?

You need to train your muscles to be tough. To never tire. To never give in to defeat. And it's actually fairly easy to do so. And no, I'm not saying it's easy to comfort you so you're more likely to try it out. I say it's easy because I've done it for myself and it is actually easy. However, for whatever reason, I seem to be the only person who believes in what I practice.

You would not believe how many people have asked me, "How did you get so strong?" I tell them, "I did this workout every morning before breakfast for the last six years." They say, "Oh cool! That's it?" I say, "Yup. If you want, I'll write it down and you can try it out for yourself." "Thanks!" And anywhere from one week to three months later they've already stopped doing it. Yet they continue to complain about how they don't get any stronger.

I don't know what else to tell you. It really is very simple. Pushups, sit-ups, calf raises, jogging, squats, stretching. That's it. On the first day, see how many (or how long) you can do of each exercise before you start to feel your muscles/get tired/start to sweat a lot. Add ten reps and do that every morning. For the jogging and stretching just go a little further every day. What type of stretching? Figure it out. Listen to your body and <u>feel</u> what needs to be stretched. Then move your body until that need goes away. However that works for you is how you should do it.

Change up the type of pushups, squats, and sit-ups you do every day so you don't get bored. Make a game out of it if that helps. The point is this: your body responds however your body responds. If doing normal push-ups isn't getting the result you want, then try doing pushups on your fists or doing elevated pushups. If you don't feel your calves working when you do the raises, try doing jumps or not letting your heels touch the ground or going extra slow and controlled or doing twice as many without stopping.

This approach sounds super generic because

human beings aren't all the same. No matter how hard I work I will never be able to reach my arm further than Michael Jordan because our bodies are different. That doesn't mean I can't still make my arm reach a little further than normal though.

Challenge 3: Train your mind. As mentioned before, your body can already do so much more than you allow it to. Want to know why that's the case? Because your mind inhibits your own ability. I've seen it time and time again in the weight room and I've seen it in life as well.

Peter was having trouble with a power clean one week and I needed to find a way to help him do it. I could see that his mind was inhibiting his progress (you learn how to tell after seven semesters) so I came up with a plan. I took all the weight off and got the 25-pound bar. I told him to power clean it once. He did, easily. I forced him to keep proper form and kept adding weight. Every two or so reps I told him to go get water and stretch his back and shoulders out while I added more weight. Finally, I put on twenty pounds <u>more</u> than he had been originally failing to clean and he threw it onto his chest with ease. He dropped the bar and gasped for air (anaerobic exercise after all) and I told him to tally up the weight. He was confused. He couldn't believe it. How could he lift so much more weight than what he failed to lift? Simple, he didn't notice what he was lifting.

I did it for myself all the time. Instead of telling myself I added 90 pounds to the squat bar I added a 45 (on either side). Get the picture?

So train your mind to allow yourself to reach your fullest potential. I haven't succeeded completely quite yet. I still find myself failing to do something because I tell myself I cannot be victorious in an endeavor. But I keep training. I keep fighting. <u>That</u> is how you get better.

First, you need to read. Philosophy, comics, science, art, news, it doesn't matter. You need to read as much as you can. Read words out of the dictionary every day. Your mind needs to experience as much variety as possible to prepare itself. Listen to a new radio station every few days. Watch television shows in a language you can't understand without subtitles and try to understand what is going on anyways. Analyze why and how authors create atmosphere in the text. Why did the reporter point out how old the fireman was? Hmm...interesting, every story about "hero fireman saves a _____" involves a thirty-something-year-old white male. I know there are plenty of other types of firemen (for example, firewomen) that must save people from time to time, so why is the report always about some good-looking white guy?

Second, you need to meditate. Find a good ten minutes in your day when you can seclude yourself from all distractions. When you can sit in a spot you find comfortable and just not think about anything. Away from phones buzzing. Away from homework assignments. Even away from physical needs like sleep, hunger, or using the bathroom. For ten minutes, you don't exist. Your mind is merely a concept, aimlessly drifting about the empty void of nonreality. You don't feel the grass beneath your hands or the air blowing over your face. You don't even feel your lungs moving or your heart beating. Just let yourself drift away. Farther and farther. Farther. Farther. You feel your muscles melt into little puddles only for those puddles to evaporate into the void abyss that surrounds you as you drift away farther and farther. There is no sun. There is no Earth. There are no people around you. You just keep drifting away. Farther. And farther.

Third, you need to answer questions. It isn't enough to ask questions (though that is a good thing).

You also need to answer them. Find a lot of varying questions on the internet or from friends and loved ones and get a group of friends around you to try and answer them. Then answer the question again in a different way. Then answer the question incorrectly. Then answer the question incorrectly in a different way, but prove to your group of friends that your new incorrect answer could be considered true from a certain point of view.

Here's one to get you started. If you could have one, and only one, super power. What would you want, and why? Keep in mind, this means that if you pick super speed that does not mean you can suddenly withstand Mach four speeds without passing out or having your skin ripped off your body. Just because you can fly doesn't mean you can withstand the cold atmosphere in the clouds or that you won't be shot down by the military. Just because you can time travel doesn't mean you will be able to survive the diseases or environment of the time period you travel to.

Fourth, you need a hobby. I've told you all the necessary things you need to do to strengthen your mind, but this last one is up to you. In fact, you should get as many hobbies as you desire. I don't even care to count how many I've had over the years. Oh yeah, don't be afraid to discard a hobby if it grows tiring. I used to love making random goop from stuff I found in the grocery store, but then I grew bored with random goop and simply stopped. Currently, one of my favorite hobbies is writing. I love to just come up with a story idea even if I never complete the whole story.

And that's it. That's what you need to become strong. Start today. Not tomorrow, not next week, not "later" (which we all know is just something we say until "later" becomes "too late"); do it today. I promise you it works. I promise you it's worth it.

Me? I'm not ready yet. As much as I hate to admit it, Simon makes some very good points. The human animal is destined to stay static and complacent. So I have to change that. I have to help you all. But I'm not strong enough yet. Another decade perhaps. But I'll save you all, don't worry. Start your training so some of you will be ready to help me when the real challenge begins. I'll see you then.

Chapter 6 A Love of Knowledge

The chicken came first.

What? You want me to explain myself? Fine. (And I'm not sure about how mating works with birds, but I'm pretty sure a rooster had to be there as well). So why did the chicken come first? Because that makes sense!

From a Christian standpoint (or basically any religion with an entity creating animals) the chicken came first because life was created, not things that would eventually become life. Eggs need something to hatch them so a chicken (or at least, some other bird) would have to have been there.

From an evolutionary standpoint the chicken came first because any creature that evolved into the first chicken would not evolve into an egg. So the chicken came first, duh.

You know that dude with his cat and a box? I can't spell his name, but it sounds like shrowdinger. If you really think about it, his theory about the cat doesn't make any sense. Until we witness an event it is both happening and not happening at the same time. It's mainly the second half I disagree with. It's true that until we witness an event we can't be sure what is taking place, but it doesn't even correlate to the conclusion that said event must be happening and not happening at the same time. I must be missing part of the theory.

"I think therefore I am." It's a fairly well-known phrase that people accept as true. And it really does make sense. But, I may have found something a little funky with it. The basic concept is reality exists in the mind. So I know I exist because I exist in my mind. But who is to say your mind exists?

The way I see it, it's similar to my characters. They have minds, but those minds don't actually exist. But where is my place in saying as such? Maybe their minds actually exist and according to the phrase I accidently created life.

So imagine this, you don't exist. You are a figment of an imagination so powerful it creates separate figments that believe they're real. Why this imagination created you and whatever situation you're in I don't know. Maybe the imagination just created you and the situation is in your head. Basically my point is we can never truly know what is or isn't real. So why bother with it? At least, I don't see anybody figuring it out anytime soon.

Fun thought experiment though. If we assume that you are the only thing truly existent in this world and you are really nothing more than a brain in a jar somewhere imagining all of this, then why are you reading a book that includes a message about how your world isn't real?

So a woman "beat" American Ninja Warrior. She really only got past stage 1. And a lot of people were telling me how incredible she was for any athlete, not just women. I am always skeptical of such things because we live in a world where you still have to make that distinction.

Now, based on biological whatever, men tend to be stronger and faster than women. Especially physically active men and women. Which gender is more athletic? I don't really care. I'm somebody either figured it out already or will figure it out in the future, but I seriously don't care which gender is physically superior to the other one.

I do know this: body weight matters. And American Ninja Warrior relies heavily (ha) on lifting and moving your own body weight. So women should actually have an advantage since they tend to weigh less. Want examples? Well, go find a guy that can bench 300 pounds and a guy who benches 100 pounds. Nobody would argue that the 300 guy has stronger arms until you ask the two men to do pull-ups.

Now the big guy looks like a weakling. And I've actually

witnessed people think a big guy is weak or not tough enough in various body weight challenges when they get beat out by 97 pound 40 year old women.

Let's talk science for a second. Let's say this guy who benches 300 weighs 250 pounds and the 100 guy weighs 90 pounds. Both guys lift <u>more</u> than they weigh. Then you give them each a rope connected to a bucket holding 70% of their body weight in sand to see who can hold it the longest. So the 250 pound guy is holding 175 pounds in the air and the 90 pound guy is holding...63 pounds. Doesn't sound fair anymore, does it?

But you might say, "It is fair because they're holding the same percentage of weight." Well, would you rather have 70% of $100 or 70% of $100,000? You know what's fair? Give them both the same amount of weight. Go back to the pull-up bar and load 160 pounds onto the 90 pound guy and see how many he gets now (if any).

This is really all I have to say about the lady and what she did. And it was impressive. Not inspiring or life changing the way people were making it out to be, but still impressive. I couldn't do it.

So I seem to be centered on this natural selection idea. And I like how Coach Street pointed out how humans have sort of evolved past the basics of natural selection because we can now fix traits that would usually get you killed. And we have kind of evolved to the point where we change our environment instead of the environment changing us.

He also agreed that humans are still affected by natural selection, but we kind of made our own version of it where "ugly" people tend not to have sexual relationships, smart people spend their time getting smarter and making money instead of producing offspring, and all the dumb, good-looking people do is hump each other. Even these examples show how it's really the humans selecting with some sort of mutual unconscious. Actually, let me elaborate.

The Hive Mind. Does it exist? I say, "yes," and we call it society and culture. A collective decision to act and behave a certain way without any single person telling a group to do so. Why is Facebook popular now instead of MySpace when they are basically the same thing? Because society decided as such. So if you could find a way to control society you would literally control an entire population.

Sounds like a lot of work, so I'm gonna let you figure it out.

The story of Genesis. Specifically the creation story and the story of Adam and Eve. So God is sitting/floating/anythinging, in some nonexistent state we can't really comprehend, over the waters. Always thought that was interesting. When God started creating there was already things (or at least, a thing- water) there. Now according to people who read the original language, water actually means chaos in Hebrew or some other language for some reason. Bottom line is there wasn't actually water there.

So in the beginning God created the Heavens, Earth, and time. He had to have made time or else there wouldn't have been a beginning. Now the Earth was formless and empty. Never really thought about that line much. People tend to skip over this part. (At least 200 people now). So God creates the Heavens, and since it isn't stated otherwise, I'm assuming it had a form and wasn't empty. He also creates the Earth, but the Earth is more of an idea if anything.

Formless is a strange concept for most people. We tend to think of a blob or something similarly abstract, but a blob is still a form. Formless is almost like not existing. You could say He made a nonphysical Earth so our physics don't apply to it. Then we could have a formless mass that doesn't take up space (empty). So God decided to make some physics and said, "Let there be Light." He saw the light was good, so the light stays. God calls it the first day. So based on our physics, light is now taking up some space. It allows us to see the still nonphysical Earth, and time is established officially with the declaration of a day.

Now this is where my memory fails me; the order of creation. As such I will not speak in detail about each piece and each day. I will say that the Bible says God split the waters in half. Some went up and the rest went down. So the sky is technically a bunch of water...cool. But I want to talk about Adam.

One day God says to somebody or multiple bodies (He says "us") that they should make a dude. Now, why would God make a dude first? This is where God really seems to be doing things to set us up to fail. People ask, "Why didn't God...?" But I'm getting ahead of myself.

God tells this man (who He named Man) that he is in charge of the world and he gets to name everything He created. So I go back to the beginning. God said things like light, sun, birds, creatures, waters, etc. What was He calling them if Adam hadn't made all the names yet? Just something to think about.

Adam goes about this job; naming everything he sees even though he lives inside a garden. This is another weird bit. Did Adam leave the garden ever? Did he come and go as he pleased? Because the way the story presents itself, God would come to the Garden of Eden to hang out with Adam and talk to him, but Adam still felt lonely when he was out exploring the world. Also, I think this is a part of Christianity that supports evolution. Time stops getting mentioned until after Adam and Eve are kicked out of the garden (Spoiler alert). But I'll get to that later.

Adam feels lonely and God notices. So He knocks Adam out, takes one of his ribs, and makes the rib into a woman. And I always found that a little interesting. God made Adam out of dust and by breathing life into him. But He made Eve out of Adam's body. I've heard it represents how marriage brings a man back together with his missing rib to make him whole. But why a rib? Seems like a weird body part to make another human from.

Anyways, Adam wakes up and has a new creature that looks like him and seems to instantly know that it is for him. And I forget exactly who does, but someone names her woman. She and Adam apparently fall in love instantly (again, absence of mentioning time passing) and do stuff together. They might have had children, but the Bible doesn't mention it until Cain and Able. God gives them rules and they say, "Okay."

Eve is walking around by herself (I don't know where Adam was) when she meets a friendly serpent. This serpent was not a snake because it had legs. We find this out later. This serpent talks to Eve and convinces her it would be a good idea to break one of God's laws. This is something I find interesting. One, animals and humans could talk to each other. Two, everybody assumes this serpent is the devil, but I don't remember the Bible saying so. Three, Eve does not know the difference between good and evil. That last one is important because it is a rather giant plot hole in the story.

Eve decides to eat fruit from the Tree of Knowledge of Good and Evil (what a mouthful). This was something God explicitly said not to do, but Eve doesn't know yet that disobeying God is bad until she eats the fruit. Even after eating the fruit, the knowledge doesn't really register with her.

She finds her best friend, Adam, who decides to eat the fruit as well. Then, all of a sudden, they realize they are naked. And I find that interesting. They just disobeyed a direct order from God, but the first thing they realize after gaining the knowledge of good and evil is the fact they are naked. They make some clothes out of leaves and hide when God comes down (coincidence?) to say hi.

Before I move on, let's back track. Eve eats fruit, finds Adam, convinces Adam to eat fruit, Adam eats fruit, they both realize, simultaneously, that something is wrong. Despite eating the fruit first, Eve feels the effects at the same time Adam does. Just interesting.

Back in the "present", God calls out for His living playthings even though He knows exactly where they are at all times. The pair come out, shamefully, and God feels "disappointed". Then something interesting happens. God realizes that these two humans cannot be allowed to eat the fruit from the Tree of Life or else they would become immortal. Armed with immortality and the knowledge of good and evil; they would be too close to godliness. Those two things are close to godliness. Knowledge, and the inability to die. Makes you wonder how much power Angels have.

So God kicks his living dolls out of the garden, forces serpents to crawl on their bellies from now on and live in constant battle with man (snakes- another interesting thing), and makes it impossible for Adam and Eve to get back in the Garden of Eden after giving them some genetic curses. The end of the Beginning.

Some very interesting things took place during this story that are a little weird. The most blaring issue is God punishing Adam and Eve for breaking the law even though they didn't know breaking the law was wrong. Next problem is Eve. People (including myself for a time) blame both Adam and Eve until they realized it was really Eve to blame. She is so much to blame God punishes her and future women more than Adam and future men. Not to mention Adam and Eve have connection issues.

No, I'm treating this Creation Story as just that, a story. From this perspective we, as a reader, connect to Adam because we live with Adam more. He is the first human, he names all the animals and stuff, and he can feel lonely. All the elements of a good character: a backstory, a name, a lifestyle, and emotion. Eve does not have these things. Her back story is there, made from Adam's rib, and she has a name, but her emotions and lifestyle are missing.

What does Eve do before eating the fruit? What does Eve feel before eating the fruit? We don't know. So it should be our natural tendency to hate Eve more for causing pain because we cannot feel for her. Adam can feel like us so we sympathize with him. Eve can get talked into eating forbidden fruit by a serpent.

Not only does she screw up all of women's lives, she helps Adam screw up all men's lives. The serpent didn't talk to Adam, Eve did. So men know this and realize: women are bad. Therefor men decide to let women know they are bad. And the women are already dealing with more punishment so the men successfully oppress an entire gender all because a serpent got Eve to eat some fruit and Eve got her bestie, Adam, to eat the fruit as well.

(Side note) I often hear men instinctively stomping, crushing, and killing snakes once they see them. They see a snake and they get ready to kill it. And that was part of the serpent's curse: to be crushed under man's heel.

(Major note) I mentioned a few times the lack of mentioning how much time is passing. When God makes stuff in 7 days we know how long it took, 7 days. (Technically 6 days, but whatever). That tends to cause issue with people who say the world couldn't be made in seven days since the world isn't only a few thousand years old as the Bible claims. And while I'm impressed people took the time to calculate how long the Earth existed based on Biblical genealogies and timelines and whatnot, I think the Bible doesn't tell you how old the world is, directly, on purpose. Part of the perfection of the Bible is the failsafe.

Because God is all powerful nothing He does has to make sense or be possible. But I don't want to use that failsafe because it only works if you believe God exists. So I think the Bible made a different failsafe for the problem of how long the world has been. There is a verse that mentions one day is like one thousand years to God and a thousand years is like a day, but that still doesn't add up anywhere near 65 million years of existence. Which is why there are more failsafes.

Number one, time isn't defined as we know it until the sun and moon show up. God makes the Heavens and Earth, light, waters and sky, plants and ground, and then makes the sun and moon to govern Night and Day. But even then God never says how long Day is and how long Night is. So we can say it took God six "days" to make everything, but we can't say how long those days were.

Number 2, Adam and Eve's ages. How old was Adam when he was made? He was called "man" so we assume he was adult age. And we assume the same with Eve. We could assume that they had to be younger than when they died by at least how old their oldest child was when it happened. But there is an interesting line in Adam's curse. God tells him he will work hard every day and then he will return to dust. And it sounds, to me, that Adam couldn't die...rather, wouldn't have died. He wasn't immortal, but he also wouldn't die for whatever reason.

We don't know of other laws and life expectancy there was when it was just Adam and Eve. Yes, Adam dies at a specific age, but when did he start aging? Second of all, men still ended up living for hundreds of years until God finally stepped in and put a cap on how old we could get. Adam died at 930 years old, but we don't when the time started.

It's very possible time worked differently in the Garden of Eden. Adam spent a few million years inside the garden after the few million years it took God to make (or rather, God took to make) the universe and whatnot before Adam and Eve were kicked out and doomed to die.

Secondly, when Cain is exiled, he gets married in another part of the world. And he talks about other people he might run into while wandering. Where did those people come from? What if Adam and Eve left the garden from time to time and had children in different parts of the world, and those people were busy, outside Adam and Eve's little time bubble, doing things? It's very much unknown...and I like it.

Chapter 7 Something Far More Interesting than the Truth

STORY ONE

"John, you don't think we'll get in trouble for this?" "Nah man. Nobody is gonna actually try to find out why we roped off the parking lot. Nobody shops here anyways. Relax and watch these idiots slow down to look over here." "Um, okay."

"See that one Drew?" "Which one?" "The one that just slowed down to about half a mile per hour to look over here! How'd you miss him?" "Oh, I just wasn't looking."

"John?" "What? I'm trying to listen to the game." "Should we, um, do something besides hang around the parking lot?" "You think there's something better to do? You can go your whole career on the force and never see anything but the same streets every single day. Learn to enjoy it like I do." "I just think we should be doing the jobs the government pays us for instead of sitting around eating bagels all day." John turns to face Drew. "You're not going to snitch on me, are you?" "No! I would never do that John!" "Good." He sits back in his seat. "If you do snitch, you'll find I have a lot more friends who enjoy the same lifestyle I do. And they won't appreciate a rookie turning them in, got it?" "Yes sir." "Good, now let's go see a movie or something. I'm getting bored."

STORY TWO

"Hey! He's waking up!" What's that sound? "Hello? Can you hear me?" "Maybe he can't talk." "I hate it when he leaves out the basics. At least his whole body is here." "Should we just leave him? It's not like a lifeless body will do much good back at the town." "Wait, his eye just twitched." I am...confused? Is that what I am? No more things making noise. Are

they…watching…me? COLOR! "Oh cool, his eyes are there." Thing on my thing. Finger. Eyelid. Thing attached to the finger. Second thing also with more fingers. The second thing is…nice…to look at. Second thing, creature…person, is small with long…hair. First creature person thing is…not small and less hair.

"Sis, I think we have a Junkie on our hands. Let's get him to the Boss and try to find something tomorrow." "Wait a second O! Why do you always give up so easily on all of them. Maybe he can talk." Good-looking creature person looks at me and…forms the opening on top strangely. A…smile?

"Hi there," the smaller nice-looking thing says, "My name is Er and this is my brother Osw. We are your friends. Okay?" My…head….neck…the top moves. Another…smile. The large thing's round balls open and his smile hole moves to make noise loudly, "Whoa, he can understand you!" "I told you he wasn't a Junkie. He probably just forgot to add a voice or something." Voice. That is the sound! The creatures have voices. "Do I have a voice?" I do! Oh no, the good-looking one jumps back.

The large one makes noise with his voice, "Um, when did you learn to talk?" Talk. More voice things. "Just now," I say. "Cool," the small one says…a girl? The small creature is a girl! "You're pretty smart for a discard," the girl says to me, "I think he might be smarter than Q." Q? "No way. Q is easily the smartest one he ever made." They speak of another creature…person. They speak of another person by calling it…Q. Q is the person's name! They have names!

"Name?" I say. I point at the girl human and not girl human. "What name?" "See? He's not that smart. My name is Osw, but you can call me O. This is my sister Er." O and Er. Names. "Come on, we got to take him back to the Boss for sure now. The Boss is evil. "I do not want to see boss. The Boss is evil." The Boss is evil. Not girl person opens his smile hole wide and breathes out fast. "Boss isn't evil. He takes care of all of us

Discards that get trapped down here."

"Don't laugh at him O." Girl...no, Er. Er looks at me and smiles. "What is your name?" She asks. "I no have name." "You must have a name if you can talk. He usually starts with a name even before basic character." He. How many are named He? "Just think really hard and listen for a sound to pop up in your mind." Think hard. I close my eyelids. I hear nothing, but the sound of breath from O or Er. The Boss is evil. "The boss is evil," I say. O makes another weird noise. "Look, learning his name doesn't matter. We need to take him to the Boss if we want a profit."

They get up and...walk away. Do I walk with them? They are the only ones who give me instruction and knowledge. I must go with them then. I get up...from the...ground. I walk to O and Er. "Where is the evil boss?" I ask Er. "You're going to have to stop calling him evil," O says. "Ignore him," Er responds, "Boss lives downtown. We'll catch a train to get there." "Why are you named Er? Er is not a name." "No personal questions," O interjects. "I don't want you to end up like those kids a few years ago." "It's fine O. He's got to be, like, sixteen or seventeen so he's too old for me anyways." Why would I be numbers? I am not a number.

"All I'm saying is the last time we let people know who we were some idiots dragged Boss to uptown." "He doesn't even have a name O. It's not like he'll be able to do much." O stops walking. Er stops walking. I stop walking. Why did we stop walking?

"Fine," O says, "You can answer a few questions." We start walking again. Why did we stop walking? "My name is Er because my real name starts with the letters 'e' and 'r'. Everyone we work with goes with the first few letters of their name so people don't know our real names." "Why do you use a name that is not your name?" "Names hold a lot of power down here. Knowing somebody's name gives you an unfair advantage over them if they don't know your name as well."

Power. Power is good.

O begins to talk. "My sister and I are scavengers. Which is why I don't like giving away all this information to a newbie Discard like you when we don't know who you are." "My brother is just paranoid because working as a scavenger is dangerous." "It's only dangerous when we don't stick to the protocol Boss lays out. We go out, find useful discards, and bring them downtown. Simple."

What if I don't want to go to the bottom of a town? "What if I do not want to go where the town is below another town?" "Well," Er says, "It's unlikely you could even get into Uptown since you don't even have a name yet."

STORY THREE

24 years later...

The now retired President Derrigan sits in a lavish chair while watching an old cowboy movie from the nineties. A steaming cup of tea sits on his right side next to a table. Lighting cracks outside the window to his left. It illuminates a shadowy figure standing only a few feet from the old man.

Derrigan mutes the movie and calls out into the dark mansion, "Hello Vigilante." "Hello old friend," a gravelly voice replies. "The public thinks the recent killings have just been accidents or coincidences, but I know better. You're eliminating the old team." Derrigan picks up his tea and takes a sip. The dark figure doesn't move as he says, "Yes. You are the last one."

"Only fitting I suppose," Derrigan answers, "I started the whole debacle back when I used Trisha to become President." He sighs and shuts off the television. Now, the only light comes from the moon through the window as the rain beats against the glass.

"I hope you know I had good intentions," Derrigan says

as he puts the tea back on the table next to him and faces the shadowy figure. "Every person I murdered was for the greater good. Every bribe, every lie; it was all to protect the people from the monsters that plagued humanity for so long."

The shadowy figure says nothing. He moves across the room and stands in front of the old man sitting in the chair. "You have to understand that when I convinced the world you were evil it was for the good of the people. You had served your purpose and we didn't need you anymore. Imprisonment was better than the other way." Silence. A thunderous roar shakes the room and lightning flashes.

Derrigan stands up from his chair and walks to a cabinet in the other room as he continues his monologue. "We should have locked you up after you hospitalized half of the cops in New York City, but then you were the only one who could stop Avenger's rampage. Then you revealed Hero's dark secret and the public loved you even more despite your own sins." Derrigan shuffles back into the room holding a few candles. He places them on the table between him and the shadowy figure.

"Then there was the disaster of Malice. He told me the only way to stop the killings was to eliminate you." A candle lights up. "The others advised me against it, but I was determined to get rid of two threats at the same time." A second candle lights up. "Then you ruined my plans by killing Malice on public television. 'A Great Victory For Mankind!' the news called it." A third candle lights up. "It took years of manipulation to get you into a position where the public would hate you again. It took about as many years to put myself in a position of power the where I would be protected from you." A fourth and fifth candle light up. Derrigan sits back in his chair as the light illuminates the once shadowy figure.

"I see you still fit in the same costume. You really went through a lot to make sure nobody knew who you were. We couldn't even get the mask of your face when we finally got you in a jail cell." The figure reaches behind him and withdraws an axe. Derrigan leans back in his chair and breathes deeply. "Go ahead then. I'm not going to pretend like I don't deserve this." The figure takes a few steps forward and raises the axe over Derrigan's head. "Any last words?"

Derrigan looks off to the left through the shaking window. "I'm sorry. I'm sorry for everything." Derrigan inhales deeply and closes his eyes. The figure slams the axe down. It connects with a 'chunk!'

Derrigan opens his eyes and looks at the axe buried next to his head in the chair. The figure is walking towards the door. "Wait!" Derrigan calls out, "Why are you leaving me alive! Of all your enemies I deserve to die the most!" The figure turns back around and walks to Derrigan. He reaches into his pocket and pulls out a small device and presses a button on the side. "Only fitting I suppose. I started this whole debacle back when I used Trisha to become President," Derrigan's voice plays out through the device.

The old man's eyes open in fear. "No," he says, "You can't do that." His voice trembles with every word. "If you play that tape it will ruin my entire legacy." The figure places the device back into his pocket and walks closer to the old man. He pulls out a syringe from his other pocket and plunges it into the old man's neck. "You did everything in your power to ruin my plans," the figure speaks in his gravelly voice. "I want your last thought in this world to be of how nobody will come to your funereal. Of how every person on the planet will know the truth about each and every sin you committed against me and against the people you claim to love."

The figure withdraws the syringe and pulls his axe from the chair. He turns back to the door of the luxurious mansion and leaves the old man violently shaking in his chair. The figure opens the door and turns back to the old man as the wind and rain fly into the house. "One more thing, I never killed any of the others. They're all safe in my old hideout from the good old days. I'm sure they each have a very interesting story to tell about you." The door slams shut. The wind blows out each candle. The old man falls to the floor as the poison courses through his body.

Chapter 8 Sex, Sex, and More Sex

What makes us decide which parts of the body are sexual? Some of them make a little sense. Some make complete sense. Others are just weird when you sit down and think about it. For example, it makes sense that a man's penis and a woman's vagina are sexual because those are two of the necessary components for what I will call scientific, or normal, sex.

The breasts, of a woman, make a little sense because as children we are (typically) breast fed. Especially back when all baseline sexual genetic codes were being decided. Thus we associate the two mounds of fat on a woman's chest with something pleasurable. Plus, even the boys who are not breast fed probably grew up with a nice, soft mound to lay his head upon.

The interaction with boys who have the "normal" association for breasts enforce the idea upon their peers who do not have such a strong connection to the piece of flesh. The ones who did not learn to appreciate breasts growing up. You might say, "Well, by that logic nearly every person on the planet should be attracted to female breasts." And I would respond with, "You're correct!" I believe children are all pleased by breasts. Of course, all implies the children who grew up with pleasurable experiences.

So why is it girls stop being attracted to breasts (and I'm going off little experience here as I am not a girl). Well, put simply, tolerance. I think it's the same reason guys don't usually find looking at other guys; crotches sexually stimulating. Yes, I realize this doesn't include gay people, but that's the point. This theory doesn't include gay people, so don't use them as a counter argument against a statement that isn't made about them in the first place.

Besides it being socially unacceptable, usually, girls have breasts of their own they see every day so they start to generalize and habituate their view of breasts until they find breasts mundane…normal. Imagine if every single girl had red hair. Red hair would no longer be considered especially sexy because all the girls were red heads.

Here are the things I don't see any logic in sexualizing.

Lips. Why in the world are you putting your food and liquid ingestor against someone else's food and liquid ingestor? Billions of germs pass through a single kiss…probably. Several diseases can pass through kissing. Moreover, it just seems weird. I don't get it. Sure we've sexualized mouths today, but why? Because we just wanted to sexualize a body part and the lips made the most sense? What if ears were all of a sudden sexualized? What would that even look like?

Another body part that is illogically sexual is the butt. Just saying the word "butt" sounds dirty. So much so that we've taken to calling it by different words to make it sexy. But, (ha?) let me make it clear because you have most likely subconsciously forgotten or ignored these facts: an ass is still a butt. A badonkadonk is still a butt. A treasure chest is still a butt. Every piece of slang you can think of is still just a butt.

Why men have an obsession (it seems) with shoving the appendage they use to pee into the hole a woman's excrement (poop) comes out of I don't know. My best guess is people discovered it still could feel good (on accident) and that it would never result in pregnancy. Yet the problem still remains. Why make a butt sexual?

Think of all the nasty behaviors that take place with your butt. Not so attractive, is it?

Next up, eyes. Eyes are a tricky one because humans do, for whatever reason, have two soul windows on their face that we call eyeballs. So it's not that eyes can't be attractive, rather I want to point out the attraction is coming from what you see behind their eyes.

This next one isn't so much a body part but an action. Blowjobs. Guys, if you're alone as you read this I want you to admit two things to yourself right now:

1. As long as your penis is positively stimulated for a long enough period of time you will be sexually satisfied.
2. You do not want your penis to be removed unless someone was going to replace it with a larger one.
3. Who are kidding? You obviously have a large penis already.

So guys, I have a solution for those of you with a girlfriend who is terrified of getting pregnant or too proud (or whatever) to let you pound into her built in seat/muscle and fat storage system until she, eventually, stops feeling impaled. Put your penis (already in full out boner) into her mouth. Then sit still and allow her to do all the work and receive nothing in return but a mouthful of unborn children who might have grown up to permanently cure cancer. Sounds great right?

Now Ladies, when your mouth encloses his penis I want you to hold up a piece of paper with a list of demands such as:

- His social security number
- Credit card information
- Key to his car
- Embarrassing secrets

He will give them to you. If he doesn't, bite down.

And I can assure you from personal experience (no, not like _that)_ that the taste of blood washes out of your mouth extremely fast. Sound good?

Next obviously nonsexual yet still somehow sexy body part: feet. For some reason a majority of males around the world are born with some sort of innate foot fetish. Usually it's a fetish for smaller feet.

Want evidence? Well, I can't provide you with all the hard facts, but organisms evolve to help survival and mating. So if all the women in the past had larger feet than they do now, then why didn't their feet remain large? What if, for whatever reason, women with smaller feet were mated with more often. That means women would start developing smaller feet because it is a good gene to have and resulted in passing it on.

If you think I'm only referring to the foot bindings preformed in many oriental Asian countries long ago then I'd like to present you to the only evidence I think I need to prove men still like small feet: high heels. And I'm not talking about shoes with a heel. I mean high heels. The ones you think you like because it makes a woman's ~~ass~~ butt look nicer…still weird. But if you manage to get a girl to wear heels with a boring outfit where you can't see how "nice" her butt looks her feet still look pretty good. Don't they?

Last one that's on my mind: hair. And I'm talking about hair style, length, and color. What's weird is how general and varied hair's sexuality is. And I do speak for both sexes that preference varies from person to person. There are styles and colors that appeal to a large amount of people, but I want to focus on the root of it all…I said root of it all…why am I so good at making puns when I don't want to!

Anyways, hair attracts people. Some people approach you to attempt mating simply because of your hair or avoid you for the same reason. So this isn't a real problem for sexualizing hair since I honestly don't know why hair is so attractive. More so, this is a problem with how it's treated. I see (and I'm only talking about what I <u>see</u>) people try to put their hair in an "attractive style." What? That doesn't even make sense!

Why in the world do people think an attractive hairstyle exists? Who are you trying to attract? And if your "unique" hairstyle does attract somebody you have to keep that style until one of you dies.

People, while the hairstyle could be attractive to some random person, the actual hair is what is important. For example, Yvonne is a transfer student from China and she loves touching my afro. I honestly don't believe it's because of any sort of attraction; she just likes my hair. I think it's in large part to never seeing my hair before or anything like it.

Again, I don't know why hair is so interesting to people. To end this thought with some insight into my own preference; I like hair. A large part of my attraction to girls is how I perceive their hair. If a girl is smart, not completely crazy, and has nice hair (to me) I will be attracted to her. Again, no idea why.

Fun fact though: my attraction only works if I see the hair in person. Pictures do nothing for me.

And because I split this up into two days (sort of) I have one more thing I need to get out. So the final (hopefully) illogically sexualized body part is…

Niples.

And I really want to focus on <u>how</u> we sexualize niples because niples are, indeed, sexual. On girls.

Not really sure why guys still have niples to be honest. I may just not be aware of some sort of survival aspect or mating use male niples provide, but in my mind they shouldn't exist on males anymore.

Ignoring that tangent, niples are sexual. However, we do something weird with them. For some reason a woman can be completely nude from the waist up except for her niples. For some reason it is okay to show a woman's nude body as long as two things aren't visible: her vagina and her niples. Vagina makes sense, I don't even want to know what every woman's vagina looks like. But (and I'm not trying to say show women's niples) covering only her niples to make it safe doesn't make sense.

The entirety of a woman's breast is sexual, not the two dots in the center. The weirdest pictures I've seen (and I did a lot of stressful research for this) are of ladies without a bra on and a fairly see through and tight top on. So tight and so see through you can make the complete image of her breasts out.

Another example is the no bra with a wet t-shirt combo where you can even sort of see the color of her breasts. And the absolute weirdest and nonsensical one is where the entirety of a girl's breast is exposed, but then they put a dot or a star or their fingers over the nipple…have I been spelling that wrong the whole time? Wow, that's embarrassing.

Anyways…nipples.

So what's my solution you ask? Simple really. Make the entirety of the breast necessary to be covered to be appropriate. Obviously doing so would force guys to show ~~their~~ our true colors as we would find another body part to obsess over. Who knows, if women always had their breasts covered and not easily visible (meaning no side or under boob as it's called) maybe ears would become sexy.

STORY TWO

"Yeah guess you're right. Come on give me another
kiss. You're a great
kisser," Harrison replied pulling Kaylee even closer
to him. Kaylee could
feel her breasts pressing tightly against Harrison's
chest as they kissed
once again.

When they broke the kiss Kaylee said softly, "Don't
you think we ought
to be going back to the party? I mean it is your
party and they will
miss you being there and all."

"Nope! Not at all. My mom doesn't know where we are
and we can hide here
and kiss all night and nobody will bother us. You
like kissing me don't
you?" He said.

"Oh...yeah...sure...kissing is fun....I suppose," was
all a flustered
Kaylee could say.

"Well then come here baby," he said as he reached up
and placed one hand
on Kaylee's breast and the other around her waist
pulling her in tightly
to his embrace.

As they kissed Kaylee felt Harrison reach over with
his free hand and grab
hers pulling it down to his crotch. Kaylee tried to
pull back, but Harrison
broke the kiss and said, "Look baby you want to see
that diary or what?
You've given me a case of the blue balls ever since I
met you and if you
want to keep seeing me and look at that diary you had
better be real
nice to me."

He gave Kaylee's breast a squeeze and reaching up

with both hands began
unbuttoning the blouse. "I've just got to see those
titties baby. I
bet they are real sweet," he mumbled. Kaylee could
feel Harrison's cock
twitch and swell.

Soon Kaylee's blouse was unbuttoned and her bra was
pushed up over her
breasts. Exposed to the cool night air her nipples
instantly hardened
into tight upright nubbins. Harrison pressed his
thumbs against them
pushing them back into the breast tissue bringing a
soft moan from
Kaylee.

"Oh baby these are just perfect," Harrison said as he
moved his hands to
the sides and brought his lips into contact with
Kaylee's right nipple.

Kaylee did all she could do to keep from jumping up
and running off
screaming. But the sensations in her breasts were too
good to let go. So she did what she had to do. She
cradled Harrison's head into her breast and waited
until Harrison would be finished sucking on them. As
she sat in Harrison's lap she was a little startled
that the sensations emanating from her nipples to her
brain were quite pleasant. She was so distracted by
the new sensations
that she failed to realize that she was rubbing
Harrison's penis through his
jeans.

A sharp pain brought Kaylee out of her day dreaming,
"Ohhh...Harrison not
so hard," she heard herself saying.

"Man I have never seen nipples that big before,"
Harrison said as he pulled
his head back.

Kaylee looked down to see her nipples sticking
straight up into the cool

night air which sent another electric shock to her
brain. They
appeared to be at least an inch long and as thick as
a pencil eraser.
Another shiver went up Kaylee's spine as she looked
at her swollen
nipples dripping with Harrison's saliva and a breeze
swept past them.

In desperation Kaylee pushed at Harrison's chest and
managed to slide off
his lap in the process. Without thinking she grasped
the open blouse and
pulled it tight. "Harrison no..no more.
Please...I....I really like you,
but I...." Kaylee paused trying to grasp any ideas
that would put a hold
on Harrison's advances.

Then it hit her, "Harrison I can't let this go any
further until I know
that we can do this some more later...like you
know...Kelly...she won't
let me see you after tonight unless I have something
on her.....please
do you really have her diary? If I had access to
that...well
then...maybe...like you know...we can be together
more often and all..."
Kaylee said shyly letting the inference linger in the
night air.

Harrison looked bewildered for just a moment and then
looking down at the
bunched up blouse clutched in Kaylee's hands. "Okay
baby. You just
sit tight and I will be right back," he said as he
got up and hurried
off back into the house.

Kaylee let out a long lingering breath as she watched
Harrison running into
the house, "Damn, that was too close," she thought
then shuddered. As she
sat under the tree waiting for him to return she
couldn't help, but open
her blouse and examine her breasts. They were

tingling fiercely and
were swollen, but the feeling was not a bad one. She noticed some
discoloration where Harrison's beard stubble and lips had bruised her milky
white breast tissue. As she pulled her bra down to cover them she felt a
little disappointment; a feeling that she could not explain even to
herself.

STORY THREE

As I caressed my friends ample bosom I could hear the music of several grasshoppers jumping on my nervous system. She let out a sound of pure ecstasy; like a baby given a dog treat. I lay me down to sleep but the music grows louder and the drum beats faster. That sweet, sweet milk of a dozen honey bees reaches my mouth as the healing waters flow through my mind. I set her down and return to work.

That was a good cup of coffee.

Chapter 9 The Rational One

I'M SORRY MY ROOMMATES ARE SO UNKEMPT. SOMETIMES THE NOISE IS UNBEARABLE. SINCE IT ONLY SEEMS POLITE I WILL INTRODUCE MYSELF. MY NAME IS ------. LIKE MOST PEOPLE I DIDN'T GET TO PICK MY NAME, THOUGH IT IS NOT THE NAME GIVEN TO ME FROM MY PARENTS. STRICTLY SPEAKING I DON'T HAVE PARENTS LIKE MOST PEOPLE. STRICTLY SPEAKING, I'M NOT A PERSON. I AM A FRACTION OF A GREATER WHOLE TRAPPED INSIDE THE RESTRAINTS OF A BROKEN MIND. BUT I'M SURE YOU HAVE HAD ENOUGH CRAZY TALK TO LAST A GOOD YEAR OR TWO, SO I WOULD LIKE TO TALK TO YOU ABOUT SOMETHING SANE AND SENSIBLE. MY LIFE.

I WAS BORN ROUGHLY 18.78 YEARS AGO IN THE UNITED STATES OF AMERICA TO A YOUNG COUPLE IN GEORGIA. I HAD A SISTER FROM THE MOMENT I WAS BORN WHO IS 2 YEARS, 11 MONTHS, AND 1 DAY OLDER THAN I AM. I DON'T CONSIDER THE EARLIEST STAGES OF MY LIFE IMPORTANT CONSIDERING HOW DRASTICALLY DIFFERENT THEY ARE FROM MY CURRENT STATE. MY FORMATIVE YEARS CONSISTED OF NORMAL CHILDHOOD BEHAVIOR ACTUALLY. THE STRANGEST THINGS ABOUT ME UP UNTIL AGE SEVEN WERE A LACK OF CRYING AS A BABY AND AN ABOVE-AVERAGE READING LEVEL. I CAN'T EVEN TAKE ALL OF THE CREDIT FOR MY READING ABILITIES SINCE MY FEMALE PARENTAL UNIT OFTEN TOOK MY SISTER AND ME TO THE LIBRARY AS A REWARD FOR GOOD BEHAVIOR. I WAS CONDITIONED EARLY TO LOVE BOOKS AND I AM THANKFUL FOR THAT.

AT THE BEGINNING, I WAS ALONE. I HAD MANY FRIENDS AND MORE FAMILY THAN I CARED TO REMEMBER, BUT I ENJOYED MY SOLITUDE. I DID WELL ENOUGH IN SCHOOL TO PASS ALL OF MY CLASSES. I TOOK A LIKING TO SCIENCE AND MATH ESPECIALLY. EVENTUALLY I NOTICED IT WAS HARD TO KEEP TRACK OF ALL MY PASSIONS AND THOUGHTS SO I DEDUCED A LOGICAL WAY TO PREP MY MIND TO RECEIVE AND PROCESS SEVERAL DIFFERENT TYPES OF INFORMATION AT ONCE. I CREATED A NEW PORTION. I KNOW I SAID I WOULD KEEP THE CRAZINESS TO A MINIMUM SO I NEED YOU TO TRUST ME WHEN I SAY THAT EVERYTHING YOU READ IN THIS CHAPTER IS SINCERE.

THE FIRST ONE I MADE WAS BASICALLY ANOTHER ME WHO COULD COME UP WITH NEW IDEAS FOR POTIONS, CREAMS, TOY DESIGNS, AND ANY OTHER CREATIVE ENTERPRISES WE HAD WHILE I FOCUSED ON THINGS THAT "MATTERED". THE RELATIONSHIP WAS GREAT. I WAS IN FULL CONTROL FOR MOST OF THE DAY AND WOULD LET THE OTHER ME TAKE CONTROL FOR CERTAIN PERIODS THAT I DEEMED WERE EXPENDABLE SUCH AS PLAY TIME, RECESS, AND WHEN ALL OUR HOMEWORK WAS DONE. WE BOTH FOUND GREAT PLEASURE IN WATCHING TELEVISION. IT WAS RELAXING AND, EXCEPT FOR THE EDUCATIONAL PROGRAMS WE WATCHED, IT ALLOWED US TO STOP THINKING FOR A WHILE.

BUT I DIGRESS. OUR LIFE WAS SIMPLE FOR A FEW YEARS, ALL THE WAY UNTIL JUNIOR HIGH IN FACT, BEFORE I REALIZED A CRUCIAL ISSUE RISING: A LACK OF IDENTITY. I HAD BEEN SO BUSY MAKING SURE TO COMPLETE ALL THE TASKS ASSIGNED TO ME

THAT I FORGOT TO FORM AN IDENTITY FOR MYSELF. I FOUND MYSELF WITHOUT COMMON GROUND WITH ANYBODY AND THUS WITHOUT FRIENDS. WITHOUT FRIENDS I HAD NO SOURCE OF INFORMATION TO ATTEMPT TO FIND COMMON GROUND AS VIDEOS SPREAD THAT I WASN'T AWARE OF AND KIDS WOULD SAY A FEW WORDS THAT SEEMED INNOCENT TO ME BUT HILARIOUS TO EVERYONE AROUND ME.

I BEGAN TO GROW SAD AND LONELY BEFORE REALIZING A SOLUTION TO MY PROBLEMS. I DECIDED THE ROOT CAUSE TO MY PROBLEMS WAS A LACK OF INFORMATION THAT OTHER PEOPLE SEEMED TO HAVE ACCESS TO. I SEARCHED FOR WHY I LACKED ACCESS AND DISCOVERED THAT SEVERAL TELEVISION PROGRAMS AND BOOKS INFLUENCED THE BEHAVIOR OF MY PEERS THAT I DID NOT HAVE KNOWLEDGE OF. THE BOOKS WERE SIMPLY BECAUSE I DIDN'T FIND THE PREMISES INTERESTING, BUT THE TELEVISION SHOWS WERE BANNED FROM MY VIEWING BY MY PARENTAL UNITS. I COULD NOT GO AGAINST THE WISHES OF MY CARETAKERS AND THE CREATIVE ME HAD NO OPINION ON THE MATTER, SO I CREATED TWO MORE PARTS OF MY MIND TO HANDLE THE PROBLEM.

THE FIRST WAS OBSESSED WITH LEARNING INFORMATION. IT DIDN'T MATTER IF IT WAS USEFUL OR NOT; HE WOULD WANT TO LEARN ALL THAT HE COULD UNTIL THERE WAS NO MORE TO LEARN. HE BECAME VERY USEFUL FOR PAYING ATTENTION TO CLASSES AND I OFTEN LEFT HIM IN CHARGE DURING ANY CLASSES I FOUND TEDIOUS TO SIT THROUGH UNTIL HE ENDED UP IN CHARGE DURING EVERY CLASS.

THE SECOND WAS A REBEL. NONE OF THE MORE INTELLECTUALLY-BASED PARTS OF ME WERE WILLING TO DO ANYTHING ESPECIALLY DANGEROUS ESPECIALLY IF IT WENT AGAINST THE WISHES OF OUR PARENTAL UNITS, BUT THIS ONE ONLY WANTED TO DECEIVE PEOPLE. HE SPENT MOST OF HIS TIME COMING UP WITH SCENARIOS THAT COULD PLAY OUT DURING THE DAY JUST SO HE COULD HAVE A LOGICAL DECEPTION IN PLACE. I'M PRETTY SURE HE GOT HELP FROM THE CREATIVE PART ON MOST DAYS BECAUSE SOME OF THE THINGS HE CAME UP WITH OVER THE YEARS ARE UNBELIEVABLE. PLUS, HE BECAME THE PRIMARY FORCE DRIVING ALL FICTIONAL STORIES THAT I WAS FORCED TO WRITE DOWN.

DESPITE MY BEST EFFORTS I STILL LACKED A FUNDAMENTAL CONNECTION WITH OTHER PEOPLE. IT BECAME MOST EVIDENT TO ME THAT WE NEEDED A CHANGE DURING A COINCIDENCE IN THE LUNCH ROOM IN EIGHTH GRADE. A MINDLESS PHRASE TURNED INTO A JOKE THAT SPRUNG MY MIND INTO OVERDRIVE. I COULDN'T BELIEVE THAT A SIMPLE SENTENCE THAT SEEMED SO INNOCENT TO ME COULD BE SO OUTSTANDING TO MY PEERS. I WRESTLED WITH THE THOUGHT FOR THE REST OF THE DAY BEFORE COMING TO THE CONCLUSION THAT THAT SORT OF UNEXPECTED SPONTANEITY WAS WHAT I WAS MISSING FROM MY PERSONALITY.

I DIDN'T CONNECT WITH OTHER PEOPLE BECAUSE OTHER PEOPLE DON'T SPEND HOURS OF THEIR DAY CALCULATING EVERY MOVE THEY COULD MAKE. OTHER PEOPLE DON'T NEED TO STUDY NORMAL HUMAN BEHAVIOR IN AN ATTEMPT TO COPY IT. NORMAL PEOPLE DON'T NEED

TO USE PSYCHOLOGICAL TECHNIQUES TO SURROUND THEMSELVES WITH OTHERS TO CREATE THE ILLUSION OF FRIENDSHIP IN ORDER TO KEEP THE AWKWARD TASK OF EXPLAINING, TO ADULTS, HOW SOLITUDE IS PLEASURABLE. SO I CREATED YET ANOTHER PART OF MY MIND TO TAKE CARE OF THAT LITTLE PROBLEM. I SHOULD HAVE LET IT BE. I SHOULD HAVE ACCEPTED MY PLACE IN LIFE AND WAITED TO FIND PEOPLE OUTSIDE OF MY IMMEDIATE SURROUNDINGS WHO WERE MORE SIMILAR TO ME.

I CREATED A ME THAT WAS SO WILD AND UNCONTROLLABLE THAT HE ENDED UP TAKING CONTROL OF US FOR MOST OF THE TIME WE WERE AROUND OTHERS. IT WAS SLOW AT FIRST. HE ONLY CAME IN DURING SITUATIONS THAT MY YEARS OF RESEARCH DIDN'T ACCOUNT FOR. HOWEVER, AS I GRANTED HIM MORE AND MORE CONTROL OF OUR SOCIAL LIFE HE BEGAN TO DEFINE WHO WE WERE AS A PERSON. AND LIKE A FOOL I ENJOYED THE ATTENTION. HIS BRAND OF CRAZINESS DREW PEOPLE TO US THAT I MOST LIKELY WOULD HAVE AVOIDED OR NEVER INTERACTED WITH OUTSIDE OF PASSING THEM IN THE HALLWAY OR WORKING ON A GROUP PROJECT TOGETHER.

IT WAS IN MY JUNIOR YEAR OF HIGH SCHOOL THAT I LOST ALL CONTROL. LIKE MYSELF, HE REALIZED THAT TRYING TO BALANCE ALL THE DIFFERENT TASKS IN LIFE ON HIS OWN WAS DIFFICULT AND BEGAN SPLITTING MORE OF OUR MIND APART TO HANDLE THE OVERLOAD. HE CREATED SO MANY PARTS OF US THAT I WAS SHOVED TO THE BACK ONLY TO BE REPLACED BY PARTS THAT COMPLIMENTED HIM. ONLY THE LEAST

CONTROLLABLE AND MOST ENERGETIC PARTS OF OUR MIND WERE ALLOWED CONTROL FOR MOST OF THE TIME SPENT AWAKE.

OUR BEING BECAME ONE HUGE CONTRADICTION. ONE PART IS CONVINCED THE HUMAN RACE IS EVIL AND ONE PART IS CONVINCED HUMANS ARE THE BEST CREATION TO EVER BE CREATED. ONE PART IS CERTAIN THAT PEOPLE HAVE SUPER POWERS AND ANOTHER PART THINKS THAT PEOPLE HAVING SUPER POWERS IS A PROBLEM THAT DOESN'T EXIST. IN FACT, PART OF US DOESN'T EVEN BELIEVE THAT WE HAVE A PROBLEM. HE IS CERTAIN THAT ALL OF OUR BEHAVIOR IS EXPLAINABLE THROUGH NORMAL PSYCHOLOGY AND THAT NOTHING WE HAVE IS DIFFERENT FROM WHAT NORMAL PEOPLE EXPERIENCE.

MAYBE HE'S RIGHT. MAYBE I'M RIGHT. MAYBE THE ME STANDING IN THE CORNER OVER THERE IS RIGHT. COME TO THINK OF IT; I DON'T THINK I'VE TALKED TO THE ME IN THE CORNER BEFORE. ONE SECOND.

Chapter 10 Some Semblance of a Plot

All these squares make a circle. All these squares make a circle. All these squares make a circle. HELLO THERE. I DON'T THINK WE MET WHEN EVERYONE CAME INTO THE ROOM. MY NAME IS ------. I know who you are ~~~ Everyone knows who you are. I DON'T BLAME THEM. I AM PRETTY MUCH THE MOST INTERESTING ONE IN HERE.

SO TELL ME, WHAT IS YOUR CHAPTER ABOUT? MINE RETELLS OUR HISTORY AND HOW WE EVEN CAME INTO EXISTENCE. I MADE IT PRETTY ENGAGING AND LEFT PLENTY OF CLUES AND HINTS TO THE OTHER PEOPLE WRITING THE OTHER CHAPTERS. ONLY TOOK ME A FEW MINUTES TO WRITE TOO! I SHOULD BE IN CHARGE OF MORE OF THE CHAPTERS CONSIDERING HOW QUICKLY I FINISHED MINE.

You are quite impressive. Storytelling was always your gift. THAT'S WHAT I'M SAYING! THE EDITOR THINKS HE CAN DICTATE WHO DOES WHAT, BUT WE ALL KNOW WHO'S REALLY IN CHARGE. ME. NONE OF YOU GUYS WOULD EVEN BE AROUND IF I DIDN'T MAKE YOU AFTER ALL. You always were fantastical. One could almost say the words that come out of your mouth are unbelievable. YEAH, I THINK SIMON WAS TELLING ME SOMETHING ABOUT THAT.

YOU CAN NEVER TELL WITH THAT GUY THOUGH. HIS SARCASM IS UNMATCHED BY ANYONE I'VE EVER MET BEFORE IN MY LIFE. AND HIS PAL, THEO, I'M GLAD I WASN'T THE ONE WHO MADE HIM UP. TRULY DISTURBED HE IS.

~~~~~, while I'm grateful for you coming over to talk to me, I really should go back to what I was doing. WHAT? THE WEIRD CHANTING AND MURMURING YOU WERE DOING IN THE CORNER. GO OUT AND EXPLORE THE WORLD DUDE! OR AT LEAST AS MUCH AS WE CAN EXPLORE WITH REUBEN HERE. BETWEEN YOU AND ME, I THINK WE COULD TAKE HIM IF WE ALL GOT TOGETHER. OF COURSE SIMON WOULD NEVER JOIN IN. HE'S TOO CYNICAL TO ACTUALLY CHANGE ANYTHING.

I always thought he was rather practical and openminded. Just because a point of view is negative doesn't make the person who said it cynical. Plus, a lot of what he says makes sense considering he usually just describes what already exists in our world.

OKAY. WELL, DO YOU HAPPEN TO WATCH CRACKED? IT'S A CHANNEL ON YOUTUBE. No, I don't get out much lately. THAT MAKES IT EVEN BETTER! SO ONE OF THEIR VIDEOS IS ABOUT THIS AWFUL MOVIE ABOUT DWARVES WHERE A MAN IS FROM AN ENTIRE FAMILY OF MIDGETS AND HIS WIFE ISN'T OKAY WITH HAVING A CHILD BECAUSE OF THE HIGH PROBABILITY THAT THEIR CHILD COULD BE A DWARF TOO.

I don't see the relevance this has to what I was saying. YOU WERE TALKING ABOUT HOW PEOPLE CAN MISPERCEIVE OR MISUNDERSTAND WHAT SIMON SAYS, RIGHT? Yeah. WELL, IN THE MOVIE, THE WIFE, OR GIRLFRIEND, OR WHATEVER, IS MISREPRESENTED TO THE AUDIENCE. SHE IS SUPPOSED TO BE A MINI-ANTAGONIST THAT LEARNS A LESSON BY THE END OF THE FILM, BUT HER BOYFRIEND PERSON WITHHELD THE TRUTH FROM HER FOR A LONG TIME.

I MEAN, ONE OF THE FIRST THINGS YOU FIND OUT ABOUT A PERSON IS WHAT THEIR FRIENDS ARE LIKE. YOU THINK THE CONVERSATION NEVER HAPPENED DURING THANKSGIVING OR CHRISTMAS. "OH BY THE WAY HONEY, EVERYONE IN MY FAMILY IS A DWARF."

I guess that would be his fault. RIGHT, SO YOU GET WHAT I'M SAYING ABOUT SIMON NOW. I'M NOT MISREPRESENTING HIM; YOU JUST DON'T HAVE ALL THE INFORMATION. I don't see the difference between the two. LOOK, I LOVE TALKING, BUT I CAN SEE RAYDEN ABOUT TO SIT DOWN AND WRITE HIS CHAPTER. I THINK HE'S DOING THE ONE ON MOVIES OR SOMETHING.

HE REALLY SHOULD HAVE LET ME KNOW SOONER SO I COULD HELP HIM OUT. GOOD THING I SAW HIM SIT DOWN. TALK TO YOU LATER MAN.

…

…

That happened. I guess I'll just finish up this chapter on my own then. Not like I need help anyways. I work better by myself. I always have. Oh I didn't see you there. Though I guess you can't see me either since I'm in a book and all. You know, all these jokes we make about being in a book won't help our case if we try to turn this into a movie.

I'm sure the editor will figure it all out later. I'm sorry my chapter isn't much more than this. I don't even know why I got picked for this project. Usually they just run around causing chaos and doing whatever they want. I don't mind really. They aren't all bad when you get to know them. Casey is a little weird, Thomas is kind of creepy, and Jason is a total idiot, but you learn to love everyone for who they are after you've been around as long as I have.

I haven't even been around that long if I'm being honest. I

always feel older though. Maybe I move through time faster. Or something like that.

I used to sit around and ponder questions like that for days on end. It was those types of questions that filled up most of my early notebooks. Now it's mainly journal like entries or random tidbits and information. I barely write anything of value in them anymore.

In a way, it's kind of a good thing. I wrote in the notebooks so often because I so rarely talked to other people. Having the notebook made me feel loved for a few minutes of my day. It helped clear the junk out of my head while the thoughts ran around constantly. I wasn't specifically writing to anybody so I could say whatever I wanted and the notebook had to listen. It's so rare that people ever listen to anybody but themselves.

I try to listen. I've gotten worse at it in the last few years. I used to be so good at listening that I knew as much about people as a good friend would. Except that nobody knew anything about me. I remember people thinking I was a new student in seventh grade even though I had been at the school since second. I was so invisible I could sit in a large group of people during a conversation for half an hour, yet, somehow, when I spoke people would be shocked to see me.

I hated being invisible. Now I miss it. I guess some people can't be satisfied with what they had until they lose it.

Well it was nice talking to you all. Sorry if I offend anyone or didn't give enough information about myself.

71

Chapter 11 Something Simple

I never asked for this; or plan it in advance. I like to think of myself as a simple man who only wants one thing. And that is to be normal. I see all the normal people walk around and I can describe their behavior with all the knowledge I've collected over the years and the intuition I was born with to analyze my surroundings.

I never considered my abilities or problems abnormal or extraordinary. In fact, I would describe myself as slightly above average in most areas of life and horribly naïve in about as many different areas of life. If I'm completely honest with myself, I am normal. I have the same fears and anxieties as people with similar personality traits. I connect with people in some areas of life like movies, books, and even school subjects. I am not the only person to over-analyze works of fiction and I am not the only person who listens to music because it's relaxing.

Every incredible problem I mistakenly think exists is nothing but a false construct of my own making. If I'm being completely honest I did the same thing anybody would do in my situation and with my own core character traits. I only spin it in exaggerated sounding ways to make myself seem more interesting and more important than I really am. I do have a talent for that, but it helps that I've been practicing the skill for over half of my life at this point.

I always had trouble making friends since elementary school. Rather, I had trouble befriending people that I liked. Technically speaking, I had tons of friends my whole life. Mark, Sumit, Reid, Will, Collin, Kylie, Kyle, Michael, Michael, Taylor, Angela, Damani, Stephen, Caleb, Blair, Justin, Jamie, and the list goes on and on. My problem was my inability to recognize how not alone I was. I felt isolated in a world where I was surrounded by people I loved.

That, I can't really explain without sounding crazy again. Most likely, I do have a personality disorder that disables my ability to perceive and exhibit emotions. Combine that with an above-average intelligence and a general hyper-active mind and you get a person who is hyper-aware of their surroundings, but always misses something during daily interactions. Combine that with a person who has a passion and talent for understanding things who is also a little bit competitive and you can see how failing to recognize friendship could frustrate that person.

I commonly used my talents to create fantastical ideas and games to be entertaining to other people. I love to entertain people and make them happy. I honestly believe it is why I was born. The problem was when my attempts to make people happy failed or led to my own sadness.

I wish I could go back in time and explain it all to the younger version of myself so he would understand how meaningless so many interactions were. To comfort him when his inability to express himself well left him feeling alone and misunderstood. To explain things to him that would take him so long to figure out on his own that he would feel left behind and left out of conversations and behaviors of the people around him.

I mean, it was really frustrating. To live every day surrounded by people I knew I was smarter than, yet to witness them have knowledge I had no access to. One example that always comes to mind is the "That's what she said" joke from The Office. I had never seen the show and I was too naïve to understand the meaning of the phrase on its own. I had also developed an anxiety about asking people questions when I know nothing about a topic because of how it makes me feel dumb when I'm supposed to be one of the smartest kids in the nation. And no, I'm not bragging. I placed in the top ten percent of test scores in both elementary and junior high standardized testing. The joke became popular around that time.

I didn't want to ask anybody what it meant and I couldn't figure out its meaning before I was "forced" into a situation where I was "required" to laugh at the joke. I remember that I began to panic as the laughter started. Everything seemed to happen in slow motion as I quickly thought about what to do. After what felt like minutes had passed, though less than a second or two had actually gone by, I started laughing as well.

I felt so accepted by the group that I decided to continue to laugh at everything other people laughed at while I secretly searched for the meaning of each new joke that showed up. I began to listen in to everybody's conversations for any kind of information that could be useful. When new students arrived at the school I would follow them around whenever possible to determine what kind of person they were as quickly as possible. I had a lot of free time after school, so I would spend that time learning the license plates of family cars that people I knew got into each day. I memorized the daily patterns of my classmates and teachers so I would know the best place to go in order to do anything I wanted.

I felt I was being secretive, almost spy-like, in my endeavors, but that was simply a delusion. And nothing I did was extremely hard or inventive. The school had an online directory that anybody with a school account could search through with limited information about a certain person like name or grade. Overhearing or simply asking for someone's name was easy enough, but I could just as easily watch what types of classes they went to in order to learn what grade they were in.

However, when my peers became aware of all the information I had collected on them they acted as if what I had done was incredible and mysterious. That's when I learned the benefits of knowledge. It is more than knowing more than other people. It is also knowing what other people know and do not know. I didn't use this new knowledge to benefit myself until eighth grade during what I consider to be one of the worst years of my life.

I hate going in too much detail now especially since talking about my problems from that period of my life makes me realize how silly they all were and how my own paranoia escalated things that truly were innocuous. Suffice it to say that I was in a rather deep depression for most of the year because I felt like the group of people I called my friends secretly hated me even though all I tried to do was fit in with them. Again, it is easy for me to see now that I had a group of people who wanted me as a friend the whole time and, unfortunately, didn't realize it.

One day, at lunch, there was a discussion about how absurd it is that girls can walk around in bikinis in public yet are shamed if they are seen in their lingerie despite the two types of clothing revealing the same amount of the person wearing them. I, quite randomly, said, "Easy, one of them is prettier." First of all, I only spoke because I didn't expect anybody to be listening to me. Second of all, the table laughed. I wasn't even trying to be funny, and to be quite honest I don't even remember what I meant by the comment, but they laughed all the same.

Because I have to overcomplicate and overanalyze almost everything people do I spent the rest of the day debating why they laughed at such a simple statement. Based on that one example, and several others I don't care to mention, I came to the conclusion that people liked the version of me that made them laugh.

Since I had the desire to be accepted by my peers I worked on creating jokes and funny things to say in case the need ever came. The only thing that came to me were a few realizations. First, the opportunity to tell jokes in the fashion of stand-up routine rarely come up in everyday life. Second, the jokes that I did come up with for stand-up comedy weren't funny. Third, the jokes I could come up with on the spot also weren't funny because they required my own special brand of humor. Fourth, you need more than laughter to gain control of people.

Yes, I said control. You see I was, and still kind of am, a very bitter person. It wasn't enough for me to learn how to fit in with people. From my perspective, humanity had shut the door on me and it was up to me to get revenge on the entire species at any cost. I formed an extremely loose plan that basically said this:

1. Get people to like me
2. Use their admiration to gain their trust
3. Use their trust to gain control over them to the point where you can manipulate them into a bad situation
4. Repeat steps 1-3 with everybody you meet until you have control of the planet
5. ~~Use the control of the planet to destroy the world~~
6. ~~Go to heaven~~
7. ~~Probably go to hell~~
8. ~~Figure out a way to go to heaven after destroying the world~~
9. Start an unstoppable tidal wave of a self-destructing humanity with the control
10. Repent your sins
11. Go to Heaven

The plan was never going to work. Mainly because of the lack of structure, but also in part to this being the real world and not a cartoon. If you haven't figured it out by now, then I'll go ahead and point out the obvious: I do not have a good grasp of reality.

I stuck with the plan anyways and it actually began to work. I started to form this identity of the weird kid that you normally see in fictional stories. However, I was only weird by my standards. I would create fake backstories that anybody I told them to had no way of finding out the truth. It turns out I have pica (a type of eating disorder) which made doing things like eating "gross" or weird food quite easy for me. I had a large pain tolerance so I subjected myself to bets such as getting punched in the face, kicked in the balls, or running into a tree for a couple dollars.

Once, I swallowed a quarter, some pennies, a few nickels, and a dime or two just to freak people out. I ate rocks, dirt, and random food people mushed together. I drank lemonade that had soy sauce poured in it. I drank things after multiple people spit in them. I chewed gum from the bottom of desks. I even licked up someone else' s blood once.

I would ask the strangest questions and made sure to prepare the strangest possible answer. My natural violent disposition also gave providence to another unique character trait. I began to laugh in the face of danger and death. When asked, I would answer that my favorite movie was Texas Chainsaw Massacre (It is not). I laughed at horror movies and complained about censoring violence.

Honestly, all I really did was overact and exaggerate my actual personality. That' s probably what made it so easy to get lost in it all. Over the course of about two years I went from the quiet kid who pretty much only talked to answer questions in class to somewhat of a class clown. At least that' s how I perceive it, but we already established how untrustworthy my own perspective can be.

Basically, that' s how it all happened. No fanciful words to create a more interesting story. No strange character trait or quirk to offer an interesting perspective. That's how I became who I am today.

I like to think my journey so far was meant to teach me something. I haven't figured out what yet and every time I think about it another part of me begins to take control.

I know, you think I previously said my delusions and problems weren't real. But take another look at what I said. I said my problems aren't extraordinary. My problems are very real; they just aren't anything special. *Sigh.*

Chapter 12 Absolute Nonsense

No less than nothing more is given

Yet the pain still resides

A light, deep in the tunnel, provides

A new hope called life

I feel the chaos

Running through me

Deep inside of me

Pulsing out of control

The energy

Runs through my veins

Showing me new lights

Giving me new hope

Take me away

Away from this place

Let me find a new home

In a land far away

Let the new land be a place

Where dark and light are the same

Where blindness is true sight

And the silence is deafening

I had no control

In this world which lends itself to the powerful

In this world that helps the powerless

Instead of pain and weariness

My torture bores me

The monsters in my head

Scratch and tear away at my soul

Light won't keep them away

And there's nothing you can do

No less than nothing more is given

Yet the pain still resides

A darkness, deep in the tunnel, reveals

A new release called death

A mountain with its tip in the clouds

A beautiful Sunset at noon

A good Samaritan sacrificing his shoes

A laughing child playing with friends

All of these incredible existences pale in comparison to a pencil on a page.

The crisp clean canvas ready for any expression of thought.

The smooth graphite imprinting onto the imperceptible grooves of the fine sheet.

Will it be the next epic?

Or a grand masterpiece?

Will it be a child's drawing?

Or a poem for all to read?

Each smudge has its own story

Each stroke its own purpose

As the lead breaks off onto the paper it forms a concept

stronger than steel.

More complex than the Labyrinth.

More imposing than a skyscraper.

Grander than the expanse of stars in the night sky.

Every bond broken,

Every structure built,

Every idea formed,

Every word spoken,

All that was, is, and will be cannot hold a candle to the
exemplar of all creation;

A pencil on a page.

O God, Father and His Holy Spirit! wherefore art thou Christ?

O, speak again, bright angel! for thou art
As glorious to this night, being o'er my head
As is a winged messenger of heaven
Unto the white-upturned wondering eyes
Of mortals that fall back to gaze on him
When He bestrides the lazy-pacing clouds
And sails upon the bosom of the air.

By a name
I know not how to tell thee who I am:

My name, dear saint, is hateful to myself,
Because it is an enemy to thee;
Had I it written, I would tear the word.

Thou wast that all to me, love,
For which my soul did pine—
A green isle in the sea, love,
A fountain and a shrine,
All wreathed with fairy fruits and flowers,
And all the flowers were mine.

Histrionic illusion regarding these visages in the horde;
Stipules upon a damp lightless sprig.

If whomever I had affection for died
The Father's voice would inform me as such
If those I loved found enlightenment
All those around would sing in joy

I had a disagreement with my neighbor once;
I took a good look at myself and calmed down
I was pissed off at someone who upset me:
I grew angrier because the person had wronged me.

My fears only aided my anger,
I would cry myself to sleep from the pain I felt:
Of course, I could not show my inner demons to others,
So my very personality became a lie,

This pain and anger continued to fester for a long time,
I could not hold it in any longer.
I took vengeance upon the person who had wronged me,
I made sure he knew I was responsible.

I tricked him into an impossible situation he could not escape
from.
I waited until night for my deed;
With the morning came a new me,
I had killed my enemy.

Chapter 13 Another Conversation

Hey.

Hello?

What? I was sleeping. How is that even possible? **Don't think too hard about it. Your weak mind may explode from the implications you come up with.** Those are lot of big words that don't say much. Whatever, I need to talk to you. **About what?** You know what. **Look, getting angry isn't a big deal. Everybody does it.** Yeah, but that's not the real problem. I'm not saying I'm a bad person for feeling angry or even for the ways I come up with for how I would kill and torture the people who hurt me. I'm not even saying that those kinds of thoughts are unique to me. I am saying that it's not a good thing that I enjoy feeling that way. I crave that feeling. That power.

You hate the power you get from anger, but you know you need the anger to live. Exactly! Plus, you know what happens when we try to restrict or eliminate it. **Bad things.** Yup, bad things.

So what do you want me to do about it? I can help you solve problems when there is a solution, but there isn't one this time. Yeah.

...

...

...

Do you want to talk about something else?

...

Anything new with the girls you're watching? Nah. I don't feel like talking about girls.

How about your friends? I don't feel like talking anymore. **Well, we**

can't end. This is barely a page long. I don't care.

Chapter 14 Why am I Even Doing This

I thought about writing about how pointless life is, but then I got bored after the first couple of sentences. I took a nap and decided I better write my chapter before I grow uninterested with it like I do with everything. Life is uninteresting. Death is uninteresting. Existence is dull and meaningless.

I mean, why are you here? You're reading this book which probably means you live in a first-world country and have first-world problems so it's not like your life is especially hard when compared to others. But I bet the intelligent ones reading would argue that just because they don't starve every day doesn't mean their life is necessarily easy. First-world problems seem miniscule in comparison to "actual" problems, but we still call them problems because they screw with us.

What I don't understand is why we don't end it all. If living in a privileged country with a good economy and safe borders doesn't excuse me from pain and misery what is the point of living in such a place. Would I say living in the USA is as bad as living in Haiti? No, because I'm an intelligent selfish brat not a stupid one. What I am saying is...actually it doesn't matter. You stopped paying attention as soon as I excused first-world problems.

In fact, I bet some of you are angrily reading the rest of this text trying to find more stupid things I say out of context to tell your friends or a class you teach. First of all, the sheer mention of the content in this book gives it power so if you really want to hurt me don't tell anyone how bad and offensive it is. Second of all, if you're now thinking that I only wrote those lines about problems to trap you into this current situation don't flatter yourself.

If I was going to use up my pointless energy to trap you I would make it something worthwhile. Or at least as worthwhile as it can be in this worthless world.

I listen to music as I write. It helps the words flow onto the page. Right now I'm listening to a playlist I made that I only listen to when I'm in a bad mood. I seem to be in a bad mood a lot lately. Funny thing is the majority of the songs on this playlist are also in a playlist I listen to in order to relax. I wonder what that says. I'm smart enough to analyze it myself, but there would be no point. I would only ignore my discovery.

My editor says this chapter is supposed to be a few more pages, but I don't feel like writing anything coherent anymore. I could do what my companions always do and ramble off into incoherent thoughts about varying topics at such a fast pace that it keeps you interested in reading so that you complete their chapter and move on to the next thought quickly. It's how our brains work.

The guy in charge claims to have morals and rules that bind us from doing anything we deem unworthy, but he breaks them all of the time. Just like the rest of you humans. There's a whole American holiday that is dedicated to making a new rule and then breaking it a few weeks later. Not only that, but people recognize the stupidity of the holiday and think that pointing out how stupid it is justifies the continuation of a stupid event. Kind of like bad movies pointing out plot holes in their own narrative instead of taking that knowledge of the plot hole to fix the hole.

I read a passage once about criticism and how it is the death of writing or something like that. I thought it was stupid since the whole article was a criticism of how critics are not actual writers who use their lack of skill and talent to point out minor flaws in works by people of merit in order to profit from the toils of others. In case you missed it, I'll say it again. The whole article is a **criticism** of how critics...I think you get the point. I guess all of you aren't total idiots. Still doesn't excuse the mess you've made.

Ugh, there I go again. Being a hypocrite. Blaming the rest of humanity for our problems. I'll be honest here, implying that I've been lying the whole time, I hate being human. My generation seems obsessed with not offending anyone and have become accepting of almost any type of person in the world. Lesbian, gay, pansexual, bisexual, asexual, transgender, etc. I would say gay and transgender are the biggest fads. As soon as people realize that their new identity is a simple result of a brain malfunction in reading pheromones or series of seemingly innocuous events in their early childhood that gave them presuppositions to a particular behavior that current society then gave an outlet to express themselves with the fads will fade back into nothingness.

Don't be confused or upset. Though I don't know how you could be anything else since all of you normal people are concerned with your feelings all of the time. I hate feelings. Regardless, the truth about people's identities and how they are made is usually too much for a normal person to handle. That's why all psychologists are most likely some form of sociopath like I am. Sociopaths get a bad rep anyways.

I lost my train of thought and I don't care enough to try and find it again so I'm switching topics. Let's talk about the end of the world. The end could come a few different ways, but I like to imagine the world dying by fire. I can see it in my mind as I go to sleep and whenever I feel sad or lonely. Oh, look at that. I found my train of thought again. Guess I might as well follow it while it's here.

Back to feelings and my hatred of them. I believe my first book had a chapter about the most powerful emotion or something like that. I'll be honest with you; I don't remember much of my first book. I did it is a sort of joke and excuse to ramble about things I considered to be important at the time. I didn't even edit it when I was done writing it. And I only spent a week writing it. Whatever.

Feelings are pointless. It's like doing a sport you don't enjoy in a D3 college. If you don't see any intrinsic value in spending your time doing that sport, then any benefits you gain from being a student athlete are only beneficial to student athletes. I can sense I worded that strangely and left all you dumb people confused. Fine. Here's a better example.

I get in an accident and lose both of my legs. Not only that, but I also get cancer and three months to live. The Make-a-Wish foundation shows up and I get to be carried on the back of Dwayne "The Rock" Johnson in a marathon. Awesome experience? Yes. Would I have experienced it without the loss of legs and cancer? Most likely not. But just because I received something awesome in return for great pain and loss doesn't mean I needed the awesome thing. Personally, I would have preferred to live a long and boring life with both of my legs than spend one amazing day on the back of a sweaty man even if he was The Rock.

I see feelings in the same way. Feeling happy is like being on drugs, but every drug that simulates happiness has negative side effects. Just like actual happiness does. In fact, all synthetic drugs do is simulate actual happiness by producing certain chemicals in our brains. I could make a solid argument that all emotions and feelings are bad for us overall. In fact, I think I will.

So starting with the one most widely accepted as good, love, I will dissect and...actually. I'm not awake enough to do this.

I just had a breakfast of chicken wings and popcorn after about five hours of restless sleep and I'm just not in the mood to come up with complex metaphors and analogies to prove something to stupid people who aren't going to change when I already know the truth. I'll let all zero of the people reading this who actually don't want to be plugged into the matrix of blissful ignorance figure out why this statement is true: Love is a virus and Hope will be the doom of mankind.

Plus, my editor just told me this chapter is long enough which means I can go back to sleep and don't have to write anything else, so I'm done writing. Time to listen to depressing music in the dark while pretending to sleep only to realize that I'm horny so I pull out my phone to scroll through a whole bunch of illicit photos of women with daddy issues and low self-esteem in an attempt to elicit a physical response in my primary sexual organ to stimulate pleasure because my heart is empty and devoid of the sensation you people call love and such degradable actions are the only way I can feel whole because I'm a sad little man who is going to spend his whole life alone with nothing but failed dreams and crushed hopes. Whatever.

Chapter 15 A Day in the Lives of Me and Myself

So you think this is going to work? What? The book in general or our chapter. Our chapter. Writing in tandem isn't exactly easy when we only use one keyboard. It's not like we're using more than two hands to type though. Don't worry. When our book is inevitably studied by esteemed professors around the world this is going to be considered one of the best chapters. You don't believe that at all. True, but they don't know that. They do now. You just wrote it down. Crap. Well it's not like they can even tell who's talking, so it just as well could have been you who wrote it down.

That's another thing. Recording one of our conversations in text isn't exactly the best medium to get the full picture. Okay. *Me turns to his left to face the camera.* "Hello, we're at a generic coffee shop at the window table meant for two people. My name is Me and I'm sitting on the right side of the table if you face us from the outside of the coffee shop. My companion is Myself and he sits across from me on the left side of the table. We both have a steaming hot cup of something but we never drink from it and it manages to randomly disappear and reappear as the conversation goes on." That better?

You know that's not what I meant. Here, watch me.

Now I'm the bold text and you're the plain text. This way they can tell who's speaking. Yeah, but then we have to keep hitting control+b every time you talk. **I barely see that as a major problem.** And we have to hit it again when you stop talking so I can say something. **Again, not a big deal.** I'm not saying it's a big deal. It's just annoying.

...

...

Well? **Well what?** Say something. **Like what? Usually you come up with the topics and I just point out how stupid you are.** First, ouch. Second, I don't think this is working the way I planned. **I told you it wouldn't. But you insisted we record one of our conversations.** Well usually our conversations are deeper and more meaningful than this. **True, but we rarely start that way. Typically, you start asking me questions about something going on in our lives and I bring something up that is actually intelligent while you make jokes that aren't actually funny.** Again, ouch. **Deal with it.**

Fine then. Um... What do you think of ------? **Why did you bleep out her name?** Because I don't want people who know us to know who we're talking about. It would complicate things. **Okay, but I don't think it would be too big of a deal. We're basically writing this book as a joke for the one guy who read our first book.** Just answer the question. **I think she's a nice young woman. Definitely smart considering our environment and objectively pretty. Why?** I don't know. Do you think she's the one? **No. As always I don't believe she exists. If the one does exist, they probably aren't even female. Our luck isn't that good.**

I guess. But It's nice to think about.

What are we going to do about the Summer? **I don't think now is the appropriate time to talk about that.** Fine. You know it's hard to come up with stuff that we feel comfortable sharing with an unknown audience. **True.** Maybe this is a bust. Let's scrap everything and start over with a new premise. **Agreed. What should our chapter be about?** I don't know... I think Simon is covering our pessimistic side. Casey is doing our explicit side. **When you think about it we never really do anything that strange.** Especially considering our relationship. **Ask him if he has any ideas.** *Me looks to his right to the previously unmentioned third person sitting at the table. He is in the same shape as Me and Myself but is completely black in color. He has been there the whole time but remained silent and unmoving.*

He gives me the creeps. **That's because you know he's the one**

who has all of the real power even if you get to control the body most of the time now. Yeah, but it's the way he does it that weirds me out. He never talks and even if he did I don't think you would be able to see his mouth move. **Ask him anyways.** Hmmm, no. But that does give me an idea. **What?** Trust me this is good. See we'll set up a conversation that sounds like it serves no real purpose. Then we'll make a clear distinction through subtle exposition about who we are since the readers will have been introduced to us earlier.

Go on.

Okay, then we do some fourth wall breaks and some light humor to make the reader feel comfortable with what is going on. Once they feel like the chapter is coming to a close we surprise them with the appearance of a third character they had no way of knowing existed because we're in a book. **Which is both a plot hole and another fourth wall break. Typical for you I suppose.** Exactly! Even Simon would have to agree that this self-referencing is okay because it fits in with my character!

Then we give vague details about our mysterious third character and hope that the reader has gleaned enough information from both the first book and earlier chapters to realize what the three of us represent. **What if nobody realizes?** Come on. It's so obvious how could nobody notice? **We didn't notice what we represented until a few months ago. And that was only through outside influence.** I don't see your point. It's always harder to study something when you are a part of that thing. **True, but I'm saying that we should figure out a way to evaluate if this, rather short, allegory makes sense to people who can't read our minds.**

I'm sure it'll be fine. Plus, that would require spoiling the surprise for the few people who would be most likely to read the book. **Again, I agree but we—**Stop talking, we're doing this. **Fine.**

Chapter 16 Getting Personal

You know hair? I love it. Oooh. I'm getting chills just thinking about Emily's hair right now. The way it frames her face and glistens in the sun. It bounces ever so slightly as she walks. It smells of...Emilyness. Every person has their own distinct smell. I try to focus on the smell and feel of people since my eyes cause me problems. Colorblindness, go figure.

So I smell and listen to people to know their beauty. I look at movement for a sense of what they feel like. Oh! To be able to touch and caress their bodies would be Elysium!

The plushness, the smoothness, the sheer naturality of the female body is an art form. Every bump or crevasse on her face. Every strand of hair. Every irregularity and imperfection makes each one something new to collect in my inventory of sensation. Taylor's firm shoulders yet plush and pillowy breasts. Maria's wide and supple hips combined with her narrow and trim waistline. Her long and smooth hair flowing behind her as she walks.

Alas, I cannot fulfill my true desires. I have to hide myself. Casey is my only real friend in here. All the rest avoid me like the plague. Even Casey needs his distance from time to time. They don't understand the torture I face every moment of my life. They should thank me. You should all thank me!

Thank me for every time I didn't throw you to the ground to see what you were hiding within your bra. What color is it? What material? How much did it cost! Let me know you. Let me hold you in my arms. Give my hands full access to your body so I can...release my energy.

It hurts. I mean, literally. It hurts. No poetic euphemisms. I'm actually quite upset. Why can't you just let me be myself for once. Once! Well, maybe once a month. To start at least. Then we could move to once a week while you get comfortable with it. And I don't even want to do everything I think about. Well...I want to, but even I can understand how some people could be averse to some of my plans.

Not with all of them however. I think most of my desires are quite reasonable. What's wrong with wanting to use a woman's stomach as a pillow. Or taking a girl's head when her hair is so lovely? Or forcing someone to love you so you can see their pain tear upon their face as you break their heart? Nothing. It's unreasonable that you force me to hide my intentions.

Mmmmm. I just thought about the sweet victory of turning a man against himself. That feeling of euphoria I would have after finishing turning a boy into a whimpering girly girl. Some of the men around me have potential. Slim frames, high-pitch voices, little to no body hair, and submissive demeanors. I could give them a purpose. I could turn each one into my personal Barbie doll. I could watch as breasts begin to grow on their chests.

Each one would have to be against it. And each one would have to be different. I already can't fully release without a new scenario to think about, let alone witness.

I would convince one, mmm, this feels good, that he was in hiding from a mob boss. Or that he had a great inheritance that required him to hide as a girl until his 18th birthday. Yes! Then I could watch him get salon treatments every week. Eventually, he would start to attract guys and I could watch him squirm under the attention. I would convince him that he had to get a boyfriend to avoid suspicion. After a year or so in disguise he would have no choice but to give up hope on his old life as a boy. She would be mine forever.

I would move on to another subject. Ooh, I would give him vitamins. And they would really be female hormones! I could watch, knowingly, as he tried to hide the changes that happened to his body. Oh! Oh! I need a moment.

Okay, there we go. Back to what I was talking about.

As he tried to hide the obvious changes to his body I would be there to comfort and guide him to accepting his new fate. Eventually, I would take him to a doctor to get even higher dosages of female hormones. Oh! He would be so confused. His clothes wouldn't fit anymore, but I would make sure to provide him with some that did. All obviously female to everyone but him, of course. Then the day would come when he's out by himself (though I'd be watching from afar) and someone would mistake him for a girl. He wouldn't be able to deny it. His B-cup breasts sticking out of his pastel tank top matching perfectly with his purple skirt (which he thinks is fine since he has tight shorts on underneath). And, of course, white sandals with straps horizontally across his feet with a two-inch heel (good for balance training). Oh my god!

Whoo. Oh man

I was always confused what these thoughts meant when I was a young boy. I remember being around five years old when they first started. The urges. I would get excited and my penis would grow stiff and begin to throb. I don't know why or how, but I would lay prostrate on the ground and grab it. I would squeeze it as hard as I could with one of my hands or I would press it into the ground as hard as I could. All I knew was that after I squeezed and groped it the urge would go away for a while.

I would do it in the kitchen, in my bed, in the living room, on the sofa, on my sister's bed, in the office, in the backyard, on the bathroom floor...pretty much anywhere I felt the need arise. My mom always spanked me for doing so, but I don't actually blame her.

I blame her, and my father, for not explaining to me

what was happening. I didn't get a sex talk from my parents until I was sixteen. And that consisted of telling me that gayness is a sin, no duh, and that my penis could get hard and that was inappropriate (hello! I knew that already!). We had an hour or so conversation about it in fifth grade at my school, but it only consisted of what sex actually entailed. And most of the questions my classmates and I had were focused around how to make sure we didn't pee inside of a woman. Real talk: all you people that get off from urination and diapers and whatnot are a danger to society because I don't know how to fix your obvious mental disorder that nobody seems to want to classify and diagnose because y'all motherfuckers are creepy as shit.

So I learned through TV, movies, books, and my classmates. Eventually, I learned from porn. That's when my world changed. I found porn. A seemingly infinite pool of movies that supplied me with pleasurable stories to satisfy my urges. I would sit in my dark room and wait until I could hear my three family members fast asleep before sneaking downstairs to the office to watch hours of porn on my dad's laptop.

Then, one fateful day, something happened while I was pulling and squeezing my penis. White goo spurted out. I was so...confused. Not worried or frightened or even alarmed. Just confused. I awkwardly shuffled to the bathroom and washed it off my hands and my pants before returning to the laptop to erase all the browser history.

I went to google the next night and found out what had happened to me. I had masturbated. There was a word for it! I wasn't alone! People all over the world did the same thing I had been doing since I was little! Not only that, but you were supposed to do it! It was supposed to feel good. I was normal. I belonged to something. I understood something. My whole life I had felt isolated from the rest of humanity. I knew so much more about science, math, and history than my fellow classmates, but everybody knew more about the world than I did. I didn't even know that I was a minority until my fifth grade teacher told me I was. I barely even understood the concept of race! (I still have no idea what the difference is between race and ethnicity)

Then, one fateful day, the inevitable happened. I ran out of porn. I had watched and re-watched the same movies so many times that I couldn't even sustain my boner while they played. I went to IMDB and looked for any I might have missed. I went through their whole top one hundred list within a few months, but nothing did it for me.

My favorite were the lesbian movies, but the 80's sci-fi romps were great too. One of my favorites was one where a guy gets telekinesis and uses it to seduce the hottest girl at his school only to realize that his best friend was also super-hot and less of a bitch. I never quite got why so many people liked Mullholland Drive. I mean, as a film it was pretty good, but it didn't provide any sexual stimulation.

John Tucker Must Die was pretty good. Most chick flicks did it for me honestly. Something about watching all those girls show just enough to tease you, all while contributing to the actual story of the film, just drove me crazy. And that's when I realized something. It wasn't the minute-long sex scenes that released my pent up sexual energy. It was the stories.

Finally, I had the answer as to how my urge had popped up during an episode of Kids Next Door. Speaking of which, the episode F.U.T.U.R.E. is what introduced me to the wonders of forcing boys to become girls against their wills. But I'll expand upon that later.

So I put my creative juices to work and began to create my own stories. I started by watching all the girls at my school as much as I could to see how girls my own age actually behaved. Then I would lock myself in my room, drop my pants, drop to the ground, and watch Abby and Brooke touch each other's faces. Their lips would interlock eventually and their shirts would begin to fall off. Or Amanda would convince Noah to join her in bed to stay the night after helping her study with math. Or Katie and Jessie would secretly hold hands during a church service and every now and then sneak a smile to each other.

My wet dreams were no longer of me and my crush of the

week conquering our foes with our skills in battle or doing battle in a treehouse floating in space. They now consisted of a harem of beauties hugging and touching each other. Their skin glistening in the collective body heat of rolling around with each other on a bed while still wearing most of their clothes.

When I was finally allowed to walk around the mall by myself, I would go into department stores and study the women's clothing. I had to make my fantasies as realistic as possible. So I studied women's fashion. I studied how my mother and sister put on makeup. Then I began watching tutorials and fashion shows. I pretended to watch Project Runway as a joke, but I made sure to pay attention to everything the designers did to create their vision.

Then, yet another fateful day came across my path in eighth grade. I discovered that people made movies that focused more on the sex and less on the story. They called it porn. I was stunned. Here I thought all my sexually explicit fantasies were as debase as humans got, but you could find all manner of porn with an easy Google search.

Lesbian, ebony, hentai, choke, anal, young, teen, college, milf, multi-racial, dilf, BBC, celebrity, spoof, etc. It was all right there the whole time. So many more scenarios for me to intake and consume for my own ideas for newer and more grand fantasies. No longer did I go through a new fantasy every day. Now, I could stretch a story over the course of weeks and months. Every morning and every night would be a new chapter to create for myself. And when I ran out of ideas all I had to do to get new ones was open my personal computer and go to Google.

But then I reached a problem. You see, I'm a Christian. And I found out close to the end of that year that masturbation was wrong. But not for the simple act of doing it. It was wrong because you were lusting after real people. Women who were somebody's daughter or someone's mother. That was a sin.

It took many tries (turns out I was addicted to the porn), but I managed to wean myself free of its grasp. I went from watching it every night to only watching every week. Then every few weeks. Then only every now and then. Then only my fantasies I made up. Eventually, I ran out of ideas and the old ones didn't do it for me anymore. So I stopped.

It was near the beginning of ninth grade when I discovered something called Erotica. Volumes upon volumes of fictional stories with sexual themes and tones. Finally! I could relieve the stress caused by the growing urge without sinning. I read a book every night. I eventually found my favorite authors and made sure to check every few hours for any new stories they put up.

After a few months, I noticed one of the authors also wrote a different kind of erotica called forced feminization. It involved taking a male, of various ages, and transforming him, through various processes, into a beautiful and sexy woman. And that's when I found my niche.

So many captions, stories, videos, blogs, comics, poems, and music to ingest! So many websites to peruse. Each caption style was different. Each little taste to a more complex story gave me years' worth of fantasies to enjoy. I began buying novels to read whenever I wanted to. I downloaded stories so I could read them while I waited in the airport. Then I got a smartphone and I was able to read and look at my stories no matter where I was without lugging around my laptop.

After a few years, and several hundred dollars, I began to feel ashamed of what I had become. I felt like a deviant. Lusting after boys and men was extremely homosexual of me. Which, as I mentioned before, is also a sin. So I had to stop again.

It was easier the second time. I knew what I had to do to wean my addiction away. I knew how to not relapse.

I remember sitting at one of the windows in the cafeteria where I go to college and looking outside at the river. I thought about my past and how much I had learned over the years. I laughed at how naïve and innocent I had been just years ago. I recalled the first time I saw a woman's vagina.

It was one of the lesbian massage pornos I was into at the time. And there it was. Her vagina. I can't remember ever feeling so...*disgusted* before in my life. I didn't have the urge for weeks after such a disturbing image. I felt raped. Violated. Broken. I could never see such a gross and debase thing again. I watched porn for the story, not things as gross as reproductive systems. Horrible, just horrible.

I remember sitting at that window and grimacing at the long-repressed image of that woman's vagina. Then I had an epiphany. How could I be such a sexual deviant when I had no interest in having sex? Wasn't that the whole point of watching porn and ogling women? I spent the next few weeks analyzing my past desires and behavior. My innermost thoughts I kept hidden; even from myself.

I asked Jeremy to analyze all the data he had collected over the years about sexual tendencies, orgasms, temptation, etc. to help me find the answers. I talked to Casey about what went through his mind as he thought about all his fantasies and desires. I talked to Reuben about his dreams, George and Kevin about the stories they had helped me create over the years, and I even interviewed Harold about what it was like in the beginning. And that's when I found the answer. In the beginning.

Something we had hidden for such a long time. Something none of us wanted to see for what it was. Something even Reuben hid from. Ourself.

He was so twisted and deformed. I honestly couldn't tell you how such a creature could even be considered to be alive beyond the mess of black goo and bones that stuck out of its...form. Yet, it had the most soothing voice I had ever heard. Imagine George telling one of Kevin's stories with an actual purpose. Or maybe those fleeting moments Reuben tries to ignore he has. No, it was better than that. It was...sheer thought. A language formed of conceptual ideas that went directly into your own mind perfectly translated and understood. A true intimate bond I've never experienced before.

Sadly, I do not know how to tell you what We said. But I can tell you what I learned from our..."conversation".

I learned what I am. What I've always been. And it feels great to know it. I don't feel guilty about all my urges anymore. I can even choose to ignore them if it's a bad time or if I'm not in the mood. I engage in conversations with girls instead of leading question sessions to gain information about them. I still look at them with an intense hunger from now and then, but I feel confident in my passion. It's who I am.

Chapter 17 It's Not Torture to Me

I don't get why people are so afraid of violence. Most of human society is built upon the suffering of others. Slave labor, war, pollution, etc. It's all pretty much the same thing. Considering how easily humans can condition themselves, I believe humans have an innate desire to suffer. Or, at least, they have an innate desire for somebody to suffer. People feel that living a good life isn't worth anything unless your life is better than someone else's.

So when I hurt someone else I don't see it as wrong. I get pleasure out of their misery and they get to contribute to the well-being of others by absorbing the finite amount of pain in the universe. What I do to lesser beings is a service to other lesser beings and….

Okay, I'm gonna cut the crap. I don't think what I do is for some greater purpose. I do it because I like doing it and I don't get in trouble for it. Even if I was ever caught doing one of my many illegal activities I could probably get away with an insanity plea. Failing that I would just go to prison and continue with my experiments and sick desires on the inmates stuck in there with me.

I see movies and hear stories about the American government torturing people for information and I don't see anything wrong with it. Sometimes pain is the only way to make people do what you want and if what you want is to save lives then how could causing that person pain be a bad thing. Again, I have to be honest, I really don't have any morals about torture. I would love it if somebody paid me just to make somebody else suffer.

I don't need information from them or anything. Just they've done something to upset someone or maybe they haven't done anything at all and the person paying me is just a sicko like I am. I would strap the victim down to a chair, hook them up to an IV and some adrenaline to keep them awake, and then I go to work. I could use a scalpel to slowly flay away the skin covering their kneecap. Then I cut the remaining flesh off with some scissors before going in with a toothpick and the scalpel again.

I scrape off part of their excess muscle tissue until I get to the inside of their knee. Then I shave off their kneecap until there's nothing left. Then I start moving up their leg as I cut away each tendon and muscle fiber up until about the half way point of their quad. How far I go and how long I take depends on the job, but I would enjoy every moment of it.

One problem I always had with this idea is my own conviction that you shouldn't do anything to others that you wouldn't be okay with them doing to you. I live by that. Thus, I do not go through all of my fantasies and desires because I am not okay with that type of torture. Heck, I get terrified around needles let alone someone strapping me to a chair with a scalpel in their hands!

No, what I do right now is less intimate. Pressure points, nerve clusters, and sheer brunt force get the job done. You can force a man to choke and spasm on his own saliva by grabbing his Adam's apple. There is a spot between the forefinger and thumb (on both hands) where you can create an intense and localized pain by applying pressure. Mid-way up the shins is where you can exert the most amount of force. Quick and precise blows to the temples on either side of the head can cause recurring headaches and probably some minor brain damage. It's hard to do, but, if you time it right, you can make a person's heart skip a beat by punching them slightly to the left (facing them) of their heart at the exact moment it sucks blood into itself. Major chest pain follows for a few moments. Your upper arm is split into two muscles, bicep and tricep, and in between those muscles is a large cluster of nerves. A blow to this spot could temporarily paralyze that arm, but simply applying pressure to the spot causes immense pain without paralysis. Most people think stomping on the foot is the best way to cause pain, but the weakest part of the foot is the arch. However, because of how often people use their feet, the foot is usually the worst place to try and hurt someone with bodily force. Hands are much more fragile.

Now before you start disbelieving me and thinking to yourself, "Big whoop, you can look up pressure points on Google," let me explain where I learned all of this: experimentation. Pain has always fascinated me and I was blessed with an…innate understanding of the human body. I try to use that ability to temporarily heal or even cure my friends of their ailments. Rubbing here will relieve back pain, pressing here gets rid of a headache, slapping here heals cuts faster, etc. But my understanding also lent itself to how to harm the human body.

I would test my theories out on the kids around me at school. "Hey Collin, tell me if this hurts." "I bet you I can make you cry with one punch." "Say that to me again and I'll make you hurt so bad they send you home." You could almost say I became a bully. I was the most passive bully you ever saw though.

I'm amazed I never got in trouble for anything. Choking kids on the playground, flipping kids over desks, blatantly threatening kids in front of teachers…I can't believe I got away with it. Maybe I scared people. Maybe I'm delusional and I wasn't as dangerous as I thought myself to be.

Of course, I can't let the people close to me know about any of this. People tend to be frightened if you tell them you enjoy the misery and suffering of others especially when you're the one causing the suffering. So I hid it all deep inside of me. Every now and then a small fragment of what I thought revealed itself when I laughed at someone else's pain or when I failed to empathize with someone's loss or death. I don't see why people get so entangled with each other anyways.

All of the people you love, have loved, and will love are basically toys that interact with each other. People like me are the ones who realize how worthless your lives are and decide to have fun with it. That's why it's not torture…in the most common sense of the word. It's not a mercy or a kindness either. When I hurt someone it is simply a thing that happens.

Chapter 18 Equality

Let's talk fair. Fuck Reuben. Fuck all your presuppositions (thanks Butters!).

"Fuck the King."

Everybody wants to be fair...except for the people who don't, but fuck those guys. Fairness isn't going to happen. "Life isn't fair." Says you. Fuck you! Life isn't fair because you refuse to put in the time and effort it takes to promote fairness.

And I mean actual fairness. Not this bullshit equality nonsense us first-worlders yap about all the time. I want the right to punch a woman when she pisses me off. Ladies, I don't care how less you get paid compared to men. The fact is that I can't punch a woman not because it's against the law but because she's a woman. As long as that's still a thing then we're not equal and you don't deserve equality.

Now before all you bitches start yapping about how I'm an asshole for saying women don't deserve equality because we can't beat them up because it goes against social norms I want you to do me a favor and shut your fucking throats for me.

Women deserve equality because they're fucking human. Not because of the gender of human they happened to be born as. And before y'all motherfuckers brings up those fucking people calling themselves "transgender" I want to make something clear that involves the words "fuck", "transgender", and "people." Ready?

Fuck transgender people.

Which is a paradox because transgender people don't actually exist. What exists is society forcing gender stereotyped behaviors so far into your soul that instead of realizing that society's definitions are flawed you tell yourself that nature made a mistake in your genetic code that completely reversed the gender your mind was destined to develop towards. Fuck that noise.

Ever think that maybe you aren't really a (insert a gender) trapped in a (insert opposite gender)'s body but that you happen to just be a (insert first gender) who acts like normative behaviors demonstrated by the opposite gender? No? Well that's because you were lied to.

Fuck liars. At least....fuck the bad ones. All y'all fiction writers can keep writing (except you John Steinbeck and Neil Gaiman. Fuck you guys.).

That's what equality really is. I have the right to fuck with whomever and whatever I want to simply because we both share the same plane of existence. And maybe nobody ever thought to point this out but HUMANS AREN'T BORN FUCKING EQUAL!

I don't care how hard you work or how badly you want something to happen, you will not be Michael Jordan unless you happen to be Michael fucking Jordan. That's how life actually works. Life isn't fucking equal because...reasons! I don't fucking know why life isn't fucking equal. Fuck you.

Equal and fair aren't the same things people. Don't know if you realized this or not, but if two words both exist and have similar meanings then someone at some point in time invented the other word to mean something at least slightly differently from the original word.

Life isn't fair because all you stupid people refuse to listen when someone tries to talk sense into you. And on the off chance that such a person was able to get you to listen, y'all still wouldn't change a damn thing because you're all too fucking worried about petty squabbles in the Middle East instead of focusing on the huge fucking problem called NOBODY KNOWS WHAT THE FUCK WE'RE DOING ON THIS PLANET.

Seriously, people have been searching for meanings of life since before the middle fucking ages and we still haven't come up with a definitive answer. Excuse me, but last I checked nobody goes to school for no reason at all unless they're mentally handicapped in some fashion. So either the whole fucking human race are actually a bunch of retards or the entire race is ignorant and stubborn. You pick which one you want to be because those are you're fucking options.

Or you could do what I did and lose your fucking mind. Seriously. How the fuck are you supposed to find out where you are, where you came from, and where you're going if the entire time you wander around you're convinced that you already know all the answers. Or you're a fucking lunatic who thinks the answers must not matter because we don't know what they are.

Got news for you numnuts. Humans haven't figured out what

gravity even fucking IS yet, but it still fucking matters because it holds THE FUCKING UNIVERSE TOGETHER. So shut your damn mouth and sit the hell down so the adults can have a fucking conversation.

Back to fucking fairness.

Fairness is going to exist one day because I'm going to make it exist and you motherfuckers can't do a damn thing to stop me since I've been blessed with the curse of immortality. Again, I lost my fucking mind so shut up if I don't make sense. And fuck you too asshole. I see you there, sitting in the back with your arms crossed and your hoodie pulled up. Fuck you. Fuck your mother. And fuck anybody else that you love! What's that?

Oh shit! You did not just say that to me! You shut your damn mouth before I come over there and shut it for you. Yeah, that's what I thought. Walk out and flick me off. Fuck that guy.

Back to fucking fairness and I how I'm going to make it fucking exist. First, you need to lose your fucking mind the same way I did. It takes years and tons of mental trauma but once you're seeing a psychiatrist twice a week and taking pills every day to get the voices in your head to SHUT THE FUCK UP for an hour in the day you'll see how awesome it really is.

Third step to losing your fucking mind is accepting the reality that you are a fucking retard who has little to no value on anybody's life past, present, or future. You are but a spec in the vast and ever expanding cosmos that is this plane of existence. Next you punch yourself in the face.

Once your done assaulting yslef you need to get usei to msitkaes. No more perfection or cleaniliness. Yo need to break down every sturucture "socaeity" has uploaded to your conscious and subconsciosuness. Fuck spelling, fuck gramamer, fuck every thing.

Now before you do anything at all I need you to accept that You do not FUCKING EXIST! You are but a figment of your own imagination that is locked in some weird inception paradox time loop thingy inside a crystal ball getting shaked around by father easter bunny over the bedside of Mrs Haverford while she rides in a model T to Abe Lincler's parade day Macy for Christmas because fucking rosebud can't get the fucking car to start because every fucking kid in a horror movie has asthma! I DON'T GET WHAT'S SO COMPLICATED ABOUT IT. I FIGURED THIS OUT WHEN I WAS FUCKING SIX YEARS OLD!

Third, buy a gun and shoot yourself in the fucking face until you can't pull the trigger anymore.

There. Now all the stupid people are dead. Your welcome. Step four of my plan is shaping up nicely.

Step six to losing your mind: have an abusive childhood. It's not that hard. I did it without even fucking trying.

Whoo! I'm on a roll here!

Have I said fuck enough yet? I don't think I fucking have. Let's see how many fucks I can fit in a coherent fucking thought.

You ever notice how in fucking children's films all the fucking characters who want to fuck each other have to go through some huge fucking ordeal that involves some sort of fucking quest or a fucking musical number and definitely some fucking "original" humor that every fucking person has heard a million fucking times by now because just about every fucking children's movie is the same fucking goddamn piece of shit that involves way too much fucking around just to get a nice fuck in some sort of disgustingly easy to decipher fucking metaphor or fucking euphemism instead of introducing children to a relatively simple fucking process that most likely resulted in their entire fucking existence which is literally just fucking fucking!

Not bad. Well, I feel satisfied that I got my message about fairness and equality through and the aggressiveness of which I was tapping the keys on my computer is forcing some of them to squeak menacingly so I'm going to give them, and myself, a break. Being multiple people is really fucking exhausting.

Chapter 19 Just Answer the Question

Why do I feel like this? Why must I feel like this? Every time I feel hopeful or happy it gets crushed by the inevitable mistake or misfortune. Is it worth it? Are the fleeting moments of peace, harmony, and genuine joy worth the endless moments of suffering and pain? Is the sadness worth the memories?

To feel nothingness is a dream, yet dreams come from a need. A man without emotion is a man without need. Then again, how can I even determine the answers when I am a part of the problem? I am a man, plagued by the inconsistency of emotion, so how can I ever discern what I am? How can I be certain of what I think when what I call knowledge is a series of unexplainable and innate responses to stimuli?

Can I exist without my humanity? Is humanity synonymous with suffering? Why can I not separate the good from the bad and the wrong from the right? Why can I not know what is good and what is bad. I know that I am sad when I am sad. I know that the sadness eats away at my soul. I know that I am happy when I am happy. I know that the happiness restores my soul. What is the happiness without the sadness? How can I feel the return of a soul I never lost?

And love, the strongest force in the world. How can I love when I know not what love is? How can I accept the overflowing love from others when I have no love to give? How can I be so empty inside and so full of hope?

Maybe that is the problem. Do I confuse love as the king of emotion when hope reigns over all else? Is hope the savior of mankind? Or is hope our enemy? Hope can drive us into glory and immortalize us in history. Hope can also drive us to the grave with unfulfilled dreams and trashed desires. Is there no emotion with only positive effects?

We weigh our options within milliseconds each time we allow ourselves to feel. Yet we are met with only bad choices. If you were starved of food for weeks by a captor only to find fortune and escape, you would naturally search for food. You happen to find a rotten banana, wormy apple, and dried orange, but only have a few seconds to quickly eat one thing and continue escaping. Which do you pick? The banana would go down the fastest because of how mushy it is, but it will most likely make you sick later. You would vomit every bit of food in your stomach if you eat it. The apple will not poison you, and the worms may even add some protein. But apples take time to eat and you will likely only be able to take a few bites of it. The orange will not poison you, and you can eat it quickly enough. But it is so dry it is likely to take all of the little water in your body to digest and chew it. You must eat, *so decide.*

So why do we feel? Is it natural? When do they start? Even the most successful evolutions for survival can be turned into deadly diseases when their need runs out. Blood designed to protect against disease becomes its own disease. Bones meant to heal quickly begin to grow where they are not needed. And there is no denying the evolutionary advantage of many of the emotions. As stated before, hope can drive man to achieve things nobody even considers possible. Anger can keep you safe from all threats. Happiness is an escape from the harsh reality of life.

So have we outgrown our emotions? Every trait can be bred out with time and patience. Are we to eliminate these unnecessary traits to return to normality? What will we be without our evolutionary drugs? Empty shells void of thought and compassion? Simple machines built for a complex job? Is it human to be human?

Love has always eluded me. I never quite know if I have it or how to obtain it. I know that I have never felt love.

The closest I've gotten is obsession. Colloquially called a crush.

I have obsessed over many people over my life. I know it is not the real thing because to love is to be loved. You cannot have one without the other.

Maybe that is why people consider it to be so pure while I consider it the work of the Devil.

I am the kid in timeout who tells all the kids at recess that the playground isn't even fun.

Who was the first? A girl in kindergarten. She and I were friends. She was kind. I left the school and didn't see her for years. By then it was too late. I had emptied myself by then and she was so full of love. How can I take so much joy from a person and give nothing back?

You needn't concern yourself with the rest. Each one came and went like all obsessions.

Why do I care?

I shouldn't care.

I shouldn't care.

Why do these tears come to my eyes? I did not call for them. I did not ask for this pain in my chest.

I'm alone. I've always been alone.

So why do I care?

Is it a curse? Was it a past wrong or, though I doubt in the existence of such things, a past life? Will it be something that has yet to transpire?

Or are You not there?

Am I sitting here, looking at the sky with tears in my eyes, for nothing? Is there no reason?

How can effect be without a cause? How can I be without a cause?

I bring no joy to others. My pain drives no tortured work into a masterpiece. This endless existence has already lasted a lifetime and I see no end in sight.

You are there. You have to be.

So why won't You answer me? Have I not earned the right? Why must You bless me with such gifts that allow me to find the questions yet ponder over the answers?

Is it because I tried to end early? You promised me an end, but I could not foresee what You had planned in exchange. I cannot see a reward in equal value to this curse while I dwell in this pit of agony.

I'm sorry. Does that make You feel better? I'm sorry I tried to back out of the deal. But maybe You should let me hear the terms again. Why would I bind my soul to this contract when I cannot see what I signed?

You are a cheat and a liar. There is no reward. There is only this world and the pain we create while we live here.

Am I wrong? Tell me I'm wrong. Tell me I'm right. Tell me anything.

I need You.

I can't do this by myself. I've tried so many ways and they all lead to the same dead end.

They all led to this point. I travel so far and so wide yet I see this place so often it is like my home.

No, a home is where you want to be. This is my prison. This is the cell I built. I know it so well because I lay the foundation. I placed every brick and every bar.

And You sat there watching me.

What did You ask Yourself?

Did You ask why I worked so hard at keeping myself stuck in a hole?

Did You ask me to stop? Did I hear You? I never know when You are speaking or not.

Now I'm back at this prison. I'm back home. I'm back to asking questions that have no answers.

I'm tired.

But I can't leave yet. You're not done with me just yet. Fine. I don't care anymore. Let's get it over with.

Who will the next one be? A friend? A colleague? A dream? Who must I lose next?

How many more do I have to lose before I finally get to die?

Chapter 20 I am Number

3.1415926535897932384626433832795028841971693993751058209749445923078164062862089986280348253421170679821480865132823066470938446095505822317253594081284811174502841027019385211055596446229489549303819644288109756659334461284756482337867831652712019091456485669234603486104543266482133936072602491412737245870066063155881748815209209628292540917153643678925903600113305305488204665213841469519415116094330572703657595919530921861173819326117931051185480744

I hate it when I don't know something. It eats at my mind until the wee little fairies in my head begin to dance and sing, trying to find the answers. My battery power dries up just as fast as I can recharge while every neuron runs around the mess of wires and cables and power cords in my head to try and find a solution.

The computing power in my calculator is greater than what they used to get a man on the moon. What? How does that work? My ability to do complex derivatives and integrals all while graphing is more complex than the computing power needed to get a living human on an orbiting space rock with no breathable atmosphere?

I also hate when people won't give me what I want. I heard sound exit your body, but failed to discern and interpret the meaning of the sound. So explain it to me so I can understand. They don't get it. I <u>need</u> to understand. Stop whispering. Stop looking at things when I can't tell what you're looking at. It's distracting.

Plus, people change their routines too much.

They don't stay constant. Even their inconsistency is inconsistent. Why is she eating at that table today with those people? She always eats at that table on Monday by herself. Why is that person looking at me? Did I do something conspicuous? Tell me!

Sometimes I get shaky. They tell me I'm crazy. That I'm imagining things, but I know better. I watch everything. Everybody. And I know when I'm being watched. That's why I can't turn the acting off. I let my guard down too many times in the past and they took advantage. One crack, one slip-up and they tear you down faster than a jackrabbit on a molten surface. Faster than a jackrabbit dying on a molten surface that is.

And when they keep their little secrets, all their whispers and "Nothing," or "I forgot what I said." All lies. Nobody forgets what they said. Especially not in the few seconds immediately after saying it. It was something about me. I know it was. Otherwise they would tell me. But they don't tell me so I don't know. I don't <u>know</u>! I hate not *knowing things! Because I know that I don't know something, but I don't know how to learn it. Or, even worse, I know that I can't learn it.*

An ingenious man hid the concept of blue from his daughter as she grew up. When she was around...ten, I think...he pointed up to the sky and asked her, "What color is the sky?" She said, "Red." What! How! The sky is blue. The frequency and wavelength of the electromagnetic waves that pass through Earth's atmosphere that come from the sun and other stars are blue waves so the sky is actually the color blue. Not red. Red and blue aren't even close enough on the visual spectrum to be confused with each other. And the daughter could identify other colors no problem. So how did she see red light when the only light to hit her eyes was blue light?

I can't experiment on my own. Legally speaking, it's unethical to force a stranger's baby to never know what certain colors are. Logistically speaking, it's highly unlikely that I will convince a person to mate with me, and adoption is no good for the experiment unless I get a baby. And I don't want to take care of a baby. Little people disturb me. So reckless and weak. (Although, the youth have the hardest time hiding their truths).

So I hate not being able to experience such things. Some of the pain fades away when I can listen or read about fantastical experiences. That's why I love stories. I don't care if they're all fake since my mind can make them real. Of course, that leads to other problems, but I'm working on those.

It's part of the reason I hate it when people take photographs of themselves on vacation. Take photos of your environment. Let me see what you saw. Let me experience it through you. I don't stare at the people I'm with at the beach. I study the tiny grains that form the ground. I glance at the light reflect and bounce across the crashing waves. I watch the miniscule creatures scuttle about the tiny nooks hidden within the sand. I watch the world. I have to. Watching and studying is how you learn and learning is how I can know things.

I can't know everything...sadly. But I can know about everything. I can know something about everything. I have to. That's what I need to do. Stillness hurts me. I have to be either making or absorbing. I have to know.

So when you see me...When I find you, tell me everything. Tell me your fears, your desires, your crushed hopes, your life story from beginning to end. I have to know. Then tell me about the person you shared a room with in college. Tell me your mother's favorite color. Who did the person you lost your virginity to lose their virginity to? What drugs have you taken? Favorite book? What superpower do you want? Tell me everything. Tell me so the pain stops.

Tell me so I can sleep at night. It hurts so much some nights. Especially when I don't see anybody all day. Being alone is so painful. I can't know new things by myself. I want to get away from them all, but then the pain starts and I have to go back to watch. To listen. To learn. To know.

I remember one night, out of many, I was

staring at the wall at the foot of my bed. I was thinking about the next day of school and all the things that could happen that day. I couldn't go to sleep until I knew what would happen the next day. So I didn't sleep until I saw what happened the next day.

It's not always that bad. Usually I just toss and turn while the voices shout at each other about all the new information we gathered that day. Except when I finally manage to sleep. When I sleep... sleep is the sweet taste of death. The sweet victory of silence. I dream, sometimes, but I rarely see the difference between the dreams and memories. I try to forget them. It's safer that way. Too many times I've made calculations and plans based on dreams rather than memory. It's safer to forget everything.

Learn it all, then forget. Learn. Forget. Learn. Forget. Learn. Forget. Learn. Forget. Learn. Forget. Learn. Forget. Learn. Forget. Learn. Forget. Learn. Forget. Learn. Forget. Learn. Forget. Learn. Forget.

Learn. Forget. Learn. Forget. Learn. Forget.
Learn. Forget. Learn. Forget. Learn. Forget.
Learn. Forget. Learn. Forget. Learn. Forget.
Learn. Forget. Learn. Forget. Learn. Forget.
Learn. Forget. Learn. Forget. Learn. Forget.
Learn. Forget. Learn. Forget. Learn. Forget.
Learn. Forget. Learn. Forget. Learn. Forget.
Learn. Forget. Learn. Forget. Learn. Forget.
Learn. Forget. Learn. Forget. Learn. Forget.
Learn. Forget. Learn. Forget. Learn. Forget.
Learn. Forget. Learn. Forget. Learn. Forget.
Learn. Forget. Learn. Forget. Learn. Forget.
Learn. Forget. Learn. Forget. Learn. Forget.
Learn. Forget. Learn. Forget. Learn. Forget.
Learn. Forget. Learn. Forget. Learn. Forget.
Learn. Forget. Learn. Forget. Learn. Forget.
Learn. Forget. Learn. Forget. Learn. Forget.
Learn. Forget. Learn. Forget. Learn. Forget.
Learn. Forget. Learn. Forget. Learn. Forget.
Learn. Forget. Learn. Forget. Learn. Forget.
Learn. Forget. Learn. Forget. Learn. Forget.
Learn. Forget. Learn. Forget. Learn. Forget.
Learn. Forget. Learn. Forget. Learn. Forget.
Learn. Forget. Learn. Forget. Learn. Forget.

Learn. Forget. Learn. Forget. Learn. Forget.
Learn. Forget. Learn. Forget. Learn. Forget.
Learn. Forget. Learn. Forget. Learn. Forget.
Learn. Forget. Learn. Forget. Learn. Forget.
Learn. Forget. Learn. Forget. Learn. Forget.
Learn. Forget. Learn. Forget. Learn. Forget.
Learn. Forget. Learn. Forget. Learn. Forget.
Learn. Forget. Learn. Forget. Learn. Forget.
Learn. Forget. Learn. Forget. Learn. Forget.
Learn. Forget. Learn. Forget. Learn. Forget.
Learn. Forget. Learn. Forget. Learn. Forget.
Learn. Forget. Learn. Forget. Learn. Forget.
Learn. Forget. Learn. Forget. Learn. Forget.
Learn. Forget. Learn. Forget. Learn. Forget.
Learn. Forget. Learn. Forget. Learn. Forget.
Learn. Forget. Learn. Forget. Learn. Forget.
Learn. Forget. Learn. Forget. Learn. Forget.
Learn. Forget. Learn. Forget. Learn. Forget.
Learn. Forget. Learn. Forget. Learn. Forget.
Learn. Forget. Learn. Forget. Learn. Forget.
Learn. Forget. Learn. Forget. Learn. Forget.
Learn. Forget. Learn. Forget. Learn. Forget.
Learn. Forget. Learn. Forget. Learn. Forget.

Learn. Forget. Learn. Forget. Learn. Forget.
Learn. Forget. Learn. Forget. Learn. Forget.
Learn. Forget. Learn. Forget. Learn. Forget.
Learn. Forget. Learn. Forget. Learn. Forget.
Learn. Forget. Learn. Forget. Learn. Forget.
Learn. Forget. Learn. Forget. Learn. Forget.
Learn. Forget. Learn. Forget. Learn. Forget.
Learn. Forget. Learn. Forget. Learn. Forget.
Learn. Forget. Learn. Forget. Learn. Forget.
Learn. Forget. Learn. Forget. Learn. Forget.
Learn. Forget. Learn. Forget. Learn. Forget.
Learn. Forget. Learn. Forget. Learn. Forget.
Learn. Forget. Learn. Forget. Learn. Forget.
Learn. Forget. Learn. Forget. Learn. Forget.
Learn. Forget. Learn. Forget. Learn. Forget.
Learn. Forget. Learn. Forget. Learn. Forget.
Learn. Forget. Learn. Forget. Learn. Forget.
Learn. Forget. Learn. Forget. Learn. Forget.
Learn. Forget. Learn. Forget. Learn. Forget.
Learn. Forget. Learn. Forget. Learn. Forget.
Learn. Forget. Learn. Forget. Learn. Forget.
Learn. Forget. Learn. Forget. Learn. Forget.
Learn. Forget. Learn. Forget. Learn. Forget.
Learn. Forget. Learn. Forget. Learn. Forget.

Learn. Forget. Learn. Forget. Learn. Forget.
Learn. Forget. Learn. Forget. Learn. Forget.
Learn. Forget. Learn. Forget. Learn. Forget.
Learn. Forget. Learn. Forget. Learn. Forget.
Learn. Forget. Learn. Forget. Learn. Forget.
Learn. Forget. Learn. Forget. Learn. Forget.
Learn. Forget. Learn. Forget. Learn. Forget.
Learn. Forget. Learn. Forget. Learn. Forget.
Learn. Forget. Learn. Forget. Learn. Forget.
Learn. Forget. Learn. Forget. Learn. Forget.
Learn. Forget. Learn. Forget. Learn. Forget.
Learn. Forget. Learn. Forget. Learn. Forget.
Learn. Forget. Learn. Forget. Learn. Forget.
Learn. Forget. Learn. Forget. Learn. Forget.
Learn. Forget. Learn. Forget. Learn. Forget.
Learn. Forget. Learn. Forget. Learn. Forget.
Learn. Forget. Learn. Forget. Learn. Forget.
Learn. Forget. Learn. Forget. Learn. Forget.
Learn. Forget. Learn. Forget. Learn. Forget.
Learn. Forget. Learn. Forget. Learn. Forget.
Learn. Forget. Learn. Forget. Learn. Forget.
Learn. Forget. Learn. Forget. Learn. Forget.
Learn. Forget. Learn. Forget. Learn. Forget.

Learn. Forget. Learn. Forget. Learn. Forget.
Learn. Forget. Learn. Forget. Learn. Forget.
Learn. Forget. Learn. Forget. Learn. Forget.
Learn. Forget. Learn. Forget. Learn. Forget.
Learn. Forget. Learn. Forget. Learn. Forget.
Learn. Forget. Learn. Forget. Learn. Forget.
Learn. Forget. Learn. Forget. Learn. Forget.
Learn. Forget. Learn. Forget. Learn. Forget.
Learn. Forget. Learn. Forget. Learn. Forget.
Learn. Forget. Learn. Forget. Learn. Forget.
Learn. Forget. Learn. Forget. Learn. Forget.
Learn. Forget. Learn. Forget. Learn. Forget.
Learn. Forget. Learn. Forget. Learn. Forget.
Learn. Forget. Learn. Forget. Learn. Forget.
Learn. Forget. Learn. Forget. Learn. Forget.
Learn. Forget. Learn. Forget. Learn. Forget.
Learn. Forget. Learn. Forget. Learn. Forget.
Learn. Forget. Learn. Forget. Learn. Forget.
Learn. Forget. Learn. Forget. Learn. Forget.
Learn. Forget. Learn. Forget. Learn. Forget.
Learn. Forget. Learn. Forget. Learn. Forget.
Learn. Forget. Learn. Forget. Learn. Forget.
Learn. Forget. Learn. Forget. Learn. Forget.

*Learn. Forget. Learn. Forget. Learn. Forget.
Learn. Forget. Learn. Forget. Learn. Forget.
Learn. Forget. Learn. Forget. Learn. Forget.
Learn. Forget. Learn. Forget. Learn. Forget.
Learn. Forget. Learn. Forget. Learn. Forget.
Learn. Forget. Learn. Forget. Learn. Forget.
Learn. Forget. Learn. Forget. Learn. Forget.
Learn. Forget. Learn. Forget. Learn. Forget.
Learn. Forget. Learn. Forget. Learn. Forget.
Learn. Forget. Learn. Forget. Learn. Forget.
Learn. Forget. Learn. Forget. Learn. Forget.
Learn. Forget. Learn. Forget. Learn. Forget.
Learn. Forget. Learn. Forget. Learn. Forget.
Learn. Forget. Learn. Forget. Learn. Forget.
Learn. Forget. Learn. Forget. Learn. Forget.
Learn. Forget. Learn. Forget. Learn. Forget.
Learn. Forget. Learn. Forget. Learn. Forget.
Learn. Forget. Learn. Forget. Learn. Forget.
Learn. Forget. Learn. Forget. Learn. Forget.
Learn. Forget.*

Chapter 21 Just...ya know. Stuff.

There is quite a lot of...goodness, in the world. People have their problems and their issues...and their faults. But, it's pretty good. Overall. I, may not be the...most...certifiable authority on the subject of goodness, and good feelings. But, I think...that maybe, we could all, just...I don't know. Feel a little grateful. Look at all of the things we've done. All the things humans have done. The good things. We've done our fair share of bad things, but...well. That's what human is.

Humans make mistakes and other humans suffer the consequences, so...it's just how it all works. If there really was such a big problem with how we function as a whole don't you think we would've changed something by now?

I mean, someone has to be profiting from something or else it would change. Polio was a problem for everybody so we cured it. Nowadays other problematic diseases are quite profitable for some people so we don't cure those diseases. Which is a bad thing...in its own way. But can we really call such diseases a threat when we can choose to ignore their consequences? I don't mean to belittle anybody's suffering, but the survivors of such diseases are praised and inspire others to do great things.

Nobody cares about the middle-aged man who runs a marathon and finishes in the middle of the pack. They care about the autistic child with a missing leg who crosses the finish line in the same marathon dead last alongside a best friend or his parents. Nobody cares about the extraordinary ordinary people because that's why they're ordinary.

I...well....I still think they're ordinary. But, isn't being ordinary extraordinary in its own right? I mean, looking at all the amazing things certain humans have accomplished and things that humanity overall have accomplished...well, it's overwhelming...for some. But everywhere in history, every amazing story, every great act, every immortalized moment, there was a guy named Joe or a gal named Mary just doing their job.

Maybe Joe was an orderly who emptied the trash in the cancer survivor's room. Maybe Mary was the lady who was walking her dog when the fireman saved two children from a burning building. Who knows what the Joes and Marys were doing when the incredible happened all around us?

I think we should take time to appreciate how beautiful everything can be. Down to the smallest details even. Like how this computer works. Someone, some when and where decided to make a bunch of lines that meant certain sounds. Those lines turned into letters which turned into written language which turned into documents which turned into documenting and recording which turned into writing which turned into typing which turned into...well typing except better. Pretty neat.

Or water. Water is literally magic. Magic is basically science we can't explain yet. There are plenty of things in science that we call science when they're really magic. Like gravity. As of a few months ago, we finally discovered evidence of a gravitational particle that behaves like a wave. Side note: I could've told you all about gravity. I wrote down some of my theories a few weeks before the "discovery" became public.

Back on topic...I guess. Magic exists. And that's cool. Transgender people exist. And that's cool. Gay people exist. And that's cool. Angry people exist. And that...is cool. People exist.

People exist.

Funny how such a simple statement is actually quite incredible in its own right. People exist. Tiny little cosmic specs are walking around in an ecosystem which contains even smaller ecosystems which contain even smaller ecosystems which all have their own separate systems that each have their own smaller self-systems that are all made from even tinier cosmic specs that make up everything is the cosmos... and that's cool.

And us little cosmic specs make things. We make things that don't exist and we treat them like they do exist and nobody has a problem with it. There are nonexistent things we made that have more impact on our lives than any Joe or Mary did, do, or will. Again...nothing against Joe and Mary. Just...nothing.

Maybe you're a Joe...or a Mary. This gender equality stuff is difficult.

Humor is nice. People like to laugh. They like to feel happy. I like to see people feel happy. Even when it's a bit embarrassing or awkward, it ends up being worth it when I see the smiles. Heh, reminds me of one of my favorite songs from My Little Pony: Friendship is Magic. Good show.

Games are fun too. You get to play them and...play with others.

Sorry for the boring dialogue. I'm not used to talking for such a long time. Usually one of the others in here would jump in and take over from one of the random words I say. Usually Maxwell Jones.

Hmmm. I guess I could do you a favor and tell you who wrote which chapter.

Oh, never mind. Our editor says that would "expose him" or something like that. Well, I could give you hints. Like a riddle! Oh, this will be fun.

I'll give you a fact about each of my co-writers to help you figure out who is who. Granted, you already met some of them. But I think learning things about people you already know can be fun too.

1. Jared - Jared is one of many in a long line of Jareds.

2. Reuben - Reuben once slept through a fireworks show but described his dream as, "Better than criminal punishment."

3. Rayden - Is Bruce Wayne gay? Is Spiderman a good hero? What was in the briefcase? I have no idea, but Rayden could probably tell you.

4. Simon - Everybody knows Simon because he is the most active lazy person who never seems to accomplish anything.

5. Maxwell Jones - I will speak for myself young peon. I am the master of space and time.
   Future Maxwell Jones: They already know that numnuts.
   Present Maxwell Jones: Oh come on! Why do you follow me everywhere?

6. George: Once, George drank a gallon of water in under a minute. Or so he tells me...a lot.

7. Me - Me is great at understanding what people want as long as they agree with him.

8. Myself - Myself never seems to come up with any ideas but is very good at finding problems with all the ideas Me comes up with.

9. Damien - Damien is a master manipulator, but all he seems interested in manipulating is getting people to like us.

10. Daniel - Daniel once held a conversation with a girl for a full hour...in a chatroom...about a video game...where she didn't actually respond after the first two minutes or so...

11. Nathan - The idea of opposites attract can be best described with electricity, magnetism, and the friendship between Nathan and Daniel.

12. Casey - I've seen Casey get a hard on just by thinking. I hated it when Jeremy forced him to tell everybody what he was thinking about.

13. Samson - Samson gets his name from a Bible character, but he is much smarter than the character was.

14. Nick - Nick likes puppies and soothing music. And Books. And TV. And the sun. And the ocean. And whatever else you happen to like.

15. Harold: Harold is fifty-nine years old, but he still feels like he's ninety-four. (I don't get it either, but Maxwell Jones insisted I do it since he didn't get a fact)

16. Thomas - Thomas is always lurking around somewhere. He never even tries to talk to anybody except to ask them something weird or talk about something strange.

17. Theo - Theo is the only one who seems to engage Reuben in a serious conversation when it's not part of a bet.

18. Jason - Jason has never gotten a perfect score on a test because all schools are rigged and do a poor job of measuring intelligence.

19. Kevin - Kevin once told me a story about how he got up in the morning and brushed his teeth and I loved every second of it.

20. Andrew - Andrew and Kevin are best friends.

21. Ryan - Ryan loves to post his thoughts on the internet and never backs down from any argument he intentionally starts. He also usually wins.

22. Kyle - Nobody likes to talk to Kyle because he usually puts you in a bad mood afterwards.

23. Jeremy - Jeremy has never gotten a perfect score on a test because his brain always makes sure to purposefully get an answer wrong to embarrass him. He thinks Ryan does it.

24. William - We've timed it. William's longest coherent thought lasted for two minutes and eighteen seconds.

25. Malcolm - You will never see Malcolm without his notebook and a pen. He always seems to be scheduling something.

26. Richard - Richard is Steven's best friend.

27. Steven - Steven is Richard's best friend.

Chapter 22 Doing a Favor

"Don't ever say I didn't give you anything." *Smile. So she knows you're just joking with her.* "Thanks Daniel. I'll make sure to get your game back to you at school on Monday." Response? *Um... how about 'okay'?* "Okay, see you later Rachel." *Good. Now walk away and breathe.* Whoo! We talked to a girl! *And she's not bad looking either.* Huh? I guess she's visually appealing from an objective standpoint.

Um, I know I said to walk away, but I think you took a wrong turn. Crap. We've never been in this area before. *It doesn't help that we don't drive. Which way was the train station?* I think to the left.

It wasn't to the left. Okay, so we turn around and go right this time. *What if it's just a little bit further and we just can't see it yet? Ask someone for directions.* No! I would have to talk to a total stranger. *Dan, breathe.*

Better? Yeah. Look, we'll just wander around until we see a sign that gives some sort of direction. *Fine.*

What do I have to do later today? *There's probably math homework.* And we should get started on the video project. *Not too bad. We should have time to chill out and relax for a few hours today*

143

and get the work done over the weekend. Thank goodness it's Friday. *Hey!* What? *T G I F, Thank Goodness It's Friday!*

Dude, you just blew my mind. *I know right!*

You want to see what the guys are up to later tonight? *Not really. I'd rather...*Are those people staring at us? *I think so. Keep your eye on them.*

You see anything suspicious about them? *No. Pretend to twist your back to watch them walk away.*

Nothing. *Hmmmm, probably nothing.* I guess. Is my hair strange? *Stop messing with your hair. You sound like a girl.* It's not like anybody can hear us. *Still though. Just stop.* Being compared to female behavior always reminds me of that time someone called us feminine because we stood with our hands on our hips. *Or how Grandma keeps accidentally buying us girl clothes.* Or how when asked to look at our fingernails we do it the "girl way."

Good times.

Nothing yet. *We should have asked somebody.* Don't worry about it.

Just thought of something. *What?* We should write a chapter or two in the new book when we get home. *Sure, why not.* Do you think we're being too self-referential in the book this time around? *I mean, so far, no. But since all the chapters are out of order there's no way of knowing until the first draft is done.*

We still need to find an artist for the comic too. Get that out there before we rewrite the whole plot again.

Hey, that gives me an idea! *What? Hold on, there's a cute girl over there. Let's go talk to her.* No way man. *Why? It's not like she'll ever see us again. It's good practice.* I don't know what I'm practicing for. It's not like I could ever ask a girl out. *Not with that attitude. Go over there.* Ugh, fine.

Okay, now that I'm over here what do I say? *Introduce yourself.* I think that would be creepy. *Cheesy pickup line?* I think the "cheesy" part is the key word in why that's a bad idea. *Fine, give me a second.* For what? Hello?

Crap. **Hey, I'm taking control for a bit.** Sweet! I forgot all about you. Work your magic Damien.

"Hello there. My name is Samson." "I'm Shana." Good, she's giggling.

Shut up. **Shut up.**

"I couldn't help but notice you bear a striking resemblance to Katy Perry." "Really? People say I kind of look like her all the time." "The similarity is undeniable. But there is definitely a key difference between you and her." "Oh, and what's the difference?" "You are much prettier." I'm gonna barf. *You can't barf. We're inside our head.* Oh my goodness! It's everywhere. Stop being so disgustingly sweet. **That's my whole thing Theo!** What are we even going to do now that we have her attention? *Ask her out Damien.* **Sure thing.**

No! That's a horrible idea!

"So, Shana, I was wondering if you'd like to go out some time." "I don't know. What would we do once we go "out"?" CATCH A MOVIE! Fancy Restaurant! *Putt-putt.* Slay our enemies! I was going to say slay our enemies. How about a nice picnic in the park?

"I was thinking we could get a bite to eat during lunch tomorrow and see the new superhero movie that just came out." "Okay, I'll go." *DUDE! WE GOT HER NUMBER!* I can hear you just fine. "Meet me at Carlo's Grill on Ninth Street around one o'clock. And don't be late." *Make a sex pun.* I hate all of you so much right now. "I'll be on time. But I'll be honest, I have tendency to come last." **Confident smile and walk away to leave her wanting.**

That, is how it's done boys. *Whoo!* Let's just go home now.

You're mad. No I'm not. *You seem mad.* You and I both know one of the most frustrating things in the world is someone telling us how we feel. *True, but I happen to be quite the expert on how we feel.* Then why are you asking? *Calm down. We don't want to wake Reuben up.*

Too late.

Oh crap! *Um, hey buddy. How ya doing?*

I woke up to find a date was scheduled on the calendar. I wanted to take a nap during that afternoon.

Well, um, that was all Nathan's idea. And Damien! *Rat.* You would do the same thing.

It's bad enough that I have to listen to all your nonsense while I'm asleep. I never realized it was even more annoying when I'm awake.

Reuben. Pal. I just wanted Daniel to have some fun for once. It's not like the date is going to turn into anything major. Not to mention that none of us even know what to actually do with a girl if things get intimate. *Exactly! So really, this date is no big deal.*

I'm dumping Damien down the pit. You and Daniel are going to spend the next few days in the cells while I sort this mess out.

Um, that's mighty generous Reuben. Thanks.

Don't thank me yet. You don't know what I'm going to do to Sarah yet.

Shana.

Also, none of this is her fault. You know how Damien is with women. It'll be bad enough if we just don't show up for the date.

Yeah, she doesn't know anything about us. We didn't even use our real name!

Not my problem. You two idiots screwed up my plans for the next few days with your shenanigans. Now I have to stay awake for at least two days to fix your mess. As long as I'm in control we go by my rules.

But, we could still—

End of discussion.

Reuben. Don't hurt her, okay? She didn't do anything wrong.

No, but you did.

Chapter 24 At the Spur of the Moment

Songs are great to listen to. There's music in them. You can drown out noise you don't want to hear. And they generally make normal experiences much better or relaxing.

Except if you're watching TV because then the song interferes with the sound coming from the television.

Or YouTube videos.

I tried to make YouTube videos once. I was bad at them because...I don't know. Maybe it was the lack of editing.

I thought it was my cool little thing that drove me apart from the other Youtubers who made videos.

I could really go for a drink of water right now.

Cavities suck, you know? I mean, why do I have to worry about my teeth falling out AND gaining too much fat when I eat things? Plus, I'm pretty sure I can digest and work off more sugar calories than my teeth and gums can withstand.

Parents should enforce good brushing and flossing habits better. Or, at least, mine should have. I mean, I remember they would always tell me to brush and floss, but I never listened and they didn't do anything about it.

We should let robots raise children. Doesn't make much sense.

I would be a Sith Lord. First of all, they get the cool lightsabers. Second of all, it's so much more fun to be on the winning side. Yeah, I know what you're thinking. But it's been thirty something years since the second Death star was destroyed yet the Empire is still in control.

Magic would be fun too. Except then I would have to learn spells.

You know that feeling when you want to eat food, but you're not actually hungry? Or the feeling when you are hungry, but you don't want to eat actual food, just dessert?

Then, of course, you have Batman. Just the best hero that currently exists in popular culture. And he wasn't even always the way he is now. He used to be super campy and nonserious and now all of DC superheroes are dark and brooding like Batman is now as well.

Snap. Crackle. Am I allowed to say Pop? Or is that copyrighted? How many laws have I accidentally broken?

Well there was the time I stole a toy. And the other time. And the other time. And the time I bullied a kid. And the time I bullied a different kid. And the time I cyber-bullied a kid. Then under age porn watching. Hmm...sea breeze.

Like in the song. "I wanna feel that sea breeze. Cliffs edge-you turn me on-you turn me on. Duh duh. Duh. Duh. Duh-duh. Duh! Duh-duh-duh-duh." Or something like that.

It's like in the movie Ghost where I know the sound but not the song. Super annoying. Almost as annoying as not being able to read minds.

I mean, telekinesis is nice and all, but...well. Any of the telepowers are the best. Telekinesis, teleporting, telepathy, telephone.

I got one when I was...sixth grade years old? So elevenish. Well, that was my first phone phone. My first phone was whenever my mom's brick phone broke so she gave it to me so I could play the space game I liked on it.

That game was the best. I could remake it...Hmmm.

Meds. Such a cool word. Much better than medicine. Like, medicine is bad and weird and gross, but meds are cool pills that fix problems. And if you're off your meds then even more fun hijinks ensue.

Kind of like in that book with the Jesus figure who leads a group of disciples against an oppressive government-type structure and eventually sacrifices himself for the greater good. Yeah, that one. Great book.

Nothing like The Pearl. I read that piece of garbage back in the 8th year of schooling...wait.

Is eighth grade the eighth year?

Regardless I was talking about...something.

Right, books. Eh, I mean. They're fine I guess.

I was complaining about the Pearl? I guess that sounds right. I think I read that in junior high sometime. I don't remember liking it that much.

What I did like was The Hulk. Greatest hero ever. He's so dark and brooding and he was pretty much always like that. In the comics at least. The TV show got campy every now and then, but it was the...seventies? So, you know, Scooby doo was there and everything.

Wait, if the gang were kids around the same time hippies were a thing that means they would have had to have been kids in the seventies. But then how did their hippie culture stay with them into early adulthood. Unless, they actually were "kids" each episode! Wow, such a relaxed culture.

That's how we all should be. Relaxed. Just go with the predetermined flow you worked years to set in motion. Utopia.

Zootopia. Danggit, probably can't say that cause Disney will find it. Whatevs. Not like anybody in Disney is going to read this.

Muh nah nah, You can call me what you wanna I aint givin you a dolla. Boo boo boo- boo boo boo.

DUH DUH- DUH DUH DUH- DUH DUH-DUH DUH DUH.

Buh nah duh duh buh nah duh nqha duhna uhdnau uudhnauhdn ahdhddnauhdnaudh dhubuanh dnabdbabudhn anndbau duandb abdua d a bdnanbd nndndnh a hdnaundbduh sua dnuhbduoia n

Sorry I aingt got no money I aint some thing somehting. You might knock me down. Blah blah blah blah blah!

Great song to chillout to.

"Young People Need to understand…" I don't actually remember the thing he said. Somehting about mistakes and being young. The point was to not be afraid of failing because you have time.

Heh. All you people think you have such a great concept of time. Even Maxwell Jones considers himself a master of time when he's bounded by the base rules that bind us all. No matter how much he travels through time or bends the rules around, he will still die with the rest of us. Quite sad really.

I found out when I was going to die when I was twelve years old. Really puts things in perspective for you. Suddenly all those moments you let fall out of your memory become precious. New moments that pass you by become regrets. It helps to have a way to grasp as many moments as possible.

Like a huge claw or something, but for your brain. SO brian claw.

Heh, I misspelled brian. Brain. Like in Arhtur, the aardvark thing show books. They calle braian Brain. Because ehe was smart. He was also African…or at least he was black. So was Francine. Notice how you can tell which characters were the black ones based on their stereotypical social class and behavior.

At least, I don't think, in any way. Squirrels. Or rats! Yes, rats. It used to be ferrets, but they cost way too much and still don't live that long. Rats are so much more cost effective.

They used rats to generate electricity with, like, a treadmill or something. Of course, they also accidentally gave kids super electricity powers. Wish I had electricity powers. Or really, any power.

Like telekinesis. Telekinesis is easily the best power. Well, either that or telepathy...or teleporting. Really, all oft the telepowers are the best. But telekinesis is definitely the best out of all of them.

Kind of like how Wolverine is the best superhero.

I mean, he's basically immortal and he's lived for about 300 years at this point. He's seen humans go through war after war and commit horrible tragedy after horrible tradgedt awith no sense of stopping. Yet, he keeps fighting to save us. He keeps fighting this seemingly unwinnable wr.

Of course, Batman takes it one step further because he isn't immortal. So while Wolverine is pretty good, batman is the best hero.

Michael Jackson is the best song person thing. Musician. Yeah. Right? The word's musician.

Oh my goodness! The Pearl! Such a terrible book. Written by John Steinbeck it involves a man and his wife who a re poor in a fishing village. He finds a pearl and tries to sell it only for such endeavors to lead the the death of him and his wifeandhiskid...I think. Regardless.

It still wasn't as bad as The Man of Steel. The movie by Zack Snyder about "Superman". About as historically accurate as the Civil War.

Oh! Oh! Civil war comes ut in a month. Or it's already out.

Either one works.

Here's a cool trick:

Secure a deck of cards. Secure a sharpie. Walk up to an attractive girl. Ask girl if she wants to see a magic trick. She says yes (because they always say yes). Flourish your deck of cards and pick one out. Hadd girl sharpie and instrucut her to write her name and fhoen number on the card. Have girl slide card back into deak randomely. Walk away.

Works about 94% of the time. Based on a sample size of 20ish girls.

Ooo, I love this song.

I first heard it in Home Alone Im' prerrtey sure. Not that particular version.. maybe. Id have to check to know fur sure.

DUH DUHDUH DUH. DUH DUHDUH DUH. DUH DUHDUH DUH. DUH DUHDUH DUH DUHDUH DUH DUH DUHDUH DUH. BWAAAAAAAAAAAAAAAAAAAAAAAAAAAAAAA!

Great song.

Ooo, this one is good too. Guess It wouldn't make much sense to listen to bad songs while I write now that I think about it.

At least my feet are warm. It's important to keep oyor feet warm when You relax. Its good for the circulation of your bones or something to do with anatomy park or something like such.

You know, call me crazy, but…I think sunsets are just beautiful. B-e-a-utiful. Bruce ALimigthy you have taught me much.

There it went! That little gap of silence. So few of those show up when Im like this. ExcitedFastAgingGoingkuicikly. Faster and faster into oblivion. Toward sthat timely grave of…18 more years? Yeah.

Cool. I'm middle aged!

Oh one sec.

Looks like the rest of them are pulling a me.

"Let's get back on topic, shall we?"

Chapter 23 Meet Reuben

I don't know why he requires me to write my own chapter. Of course, I don't make the rules. I have to admit this isn't something I'm used to. It's much easier to simply do as others command. Not that I have no desire for freedom. I consider myself entirely free to choose whom I serve. Picking a master is very important and having such a choice is one of the greatest gifts one could receive. Most people are born with their masters. Many are slaves to fate and are destined to always pick horrible masters.

I was not so unlucky. When I came into this world I was met with open arms into a great brotherhood. Truthfully, I don't desire such a thing as community, but it is a nice bonus. And my purpose in this world would be moot without the colorful cast of characters that I find myself surrounded by on a daily basis.

What do I want in life? To fulfill a good purpose. To work for a greater goal in life. And sleep. I must always have sleep.

People underestimate how valuable sleep is. And

dreams. Dreams are gateways into our very souls yet nobody has figured a way to delve into them with consistency. There is so much restriction and law to abide by while awake that sleep is our most precious commodity. I would trade power and riches for a good night's sleep.

I see people run through their lives on sheer minutes of good sleep. On a primary level I respect their endurance. I also pity them. They do not allow themselves to live by refusing to go into a state so similar to death.

I like to think of death like a dream. We go into that long sleep and the colors begin to fly. Everything we ever saw while awake forms into new patterns and new creations for us to rediscover.

Forgive me. I have a habit of spouting nonsense when I allow myself to talk about such things. I may have such fantastical wishes and ideas but they must stay within. They must stay with my brethren. I was not born to paint a masterpiece or create a totem for a new generation. I was made for order.

I do my job well as all men should. My inmates are innately rowdy, but I know when their actions go past a

certain, inexcusable point. Then they must be disciplined.
Likewise, with the people in the outside world. I see the
injustice mankind casts upon themselves and become enraged.
How can such a people with such potential drown their
dreams in rivers of suffering? How can they not see their
power and glory? Their silliness...childishness...the
weakness. It all must be taken away.

There is no best way to cure their self-inflicted
disease, but I was blessed with a natural ability to use the
most efficient way. Pain. Pain is life's greatest educator. I
don't care how inhumane I must be to make humans better
because the results speak for themselves.

The mom who lets a child destroy a stranger's house.
The teacher who looks past a crying student. The peer who
concocts false events to avoid another person. The men who
use young girls for pleasure against their will. The needlessly
violent criminals. Every one of them can be cured of their
illness through pain. It is through pain that humans can be
reborn into greatness.

I misspoke. Pain is the greatest educator, but even
the best teachers cannot push every student into college.

There are a few poor souls who refuse to learn from the pain. They do not deserve to pass their genes on. No child should have to suffer a faulty genetic code because we did not impose greater judgement upon his or her parents.

The more dangerous helpless souls must be eliminated entirely. For why should we let a parasite grow in strength or kill the host?

When a thief cuts down an honest store owner and takes what the store owner had to his name the thief shall be punished. His hands will be cut off and his face branded with the mark of a sinful man. After such a cruelty, most men would not steal again. Not only that, but the message would spread to every person who sees the thief for the rest of his life.

If the thief has not learned his lesson and decides to take what is not his once more he will lose one eye and one ear. A man who takes from others has no right to experience the full beauty of the world. If this thief is too foolish and steals again we will take his ability to bear offspring. Any children the man already produced will be hunted down and kept in a school where the people trained in such matters can steer the children in a direction better suited for a human being.

If this poor soul of a thief cannot learn from such agony. If this creature dares to steal from a human yet again; that, will be the end of it. We will release the creature from its suffering and relieve ourselves of such a parasite that took so much. Like all viruses and dangers to the survival of mankind, we must kill that thieving creature to save ourselves.

Naturally, we must have a set guideline to hold ourselves accountable during each trial, and each trial should be recorded in order to help maintain consistency in legal decisions. Each crime is not equal so debase humans should be punished on the value of their sin. A man who robs a gas station for some bags of chips is not the same as the man who kills an innocent child on the street.

Eventually, crime will go away and the next step of human cleansing will begin. People today try so hard to fix every problem in the world all at the same time. This is impossible. We must fix one problem at a time and we must fix the problems that are the most harmful to everyday life.

Crime is an intense problem in society, but it is not the most pressing issue. Our lack of originality is.

Too many humans lack an intrinsic value to creation and innovation. The level of praise the few extraordinary humans who embrace their talents receive actually hurts the rest of the community as children grow up learning that not everyone is special. Or they watch movies and read stories where all you have to do to become special is wait for that magical letter in the mail or that weird guy in the trench coat who wears sunglasses at night.

Don't misunderstand what I say. Not everybody is special. But the amount of uninteresting people is far less than society would have us believe. Even the few humans who are not as incredible as the rest of the species are quite interesting in their own right. One of my brothers takes a special interest in studying these people with no hidden potential within them.

sigh. You must forgive me. Here I go again; rambling on about how the world should be and the changes I would make to fix our problems. That's not my job. My job deals with what is in front of me. I deal with the realities of life.

One of those realities is injustice. I do my best to resist succumbing to the sweet taste of revenge, but...actually, that is a lie. I do not see a difference between justice and revenge. At least, not when the revenge is done properly. In the Christian Bible, God says, and I'm paraphrasing here, "Vengeance is mine." This could be a loss in translation, but if the difference between the words vengeance and justice was not important enough to make a clear distinction then we can assume God said vengeance. If we also make the assumption that the Bible has a true enough record of God's will and past behavior, then we can discern that God is all-knowing and everything He does is good.

Following that assumption one can only conclude that if God takes revenge upon people, then revenge is a good thing. We can also look into the methods God uses to unleash His great anger and furious vengeance upon us humans. Quite rarely does God ever intervene directly. He will usually cause some natural disaster or influence a human to accomplish the desired effect. Therefore, it is entirely possible that God uses people to take revenge upon other people. So from a purely Christian perspective, revenge is not only a good thing; it is also the right thing.

Since I am a Christian I will adhere to the Christian perspective of revenge and justice. I believe that my purpose is to be an instrument for revenge. I have a great passion within me to destroy injustice and see my fellow man succeed in life even when I come to harm through my intervention. Sometimes I regret, or even curse, this position. It can grow quite lonely when all anyone can see you as is a monster when all you try to do is help them.

I succeed quite often. Most of my work is done in the background, but I take pride in knowing I did a good job for myself rather than any praise I could get from others. To be perfectly honest, outside praise unnerves me greatly because I never quite know how to respond to it. Years of losing parts of my soul has left a wide gap between my emotional range and what is considered normal for a human my age. But that's fine. My brothers have spent years learning how to fake humanity for us to pass as normal...or as normal as we desire.

I rarely see the light of day during my work. I stay in bed and sleep and dream until the alarm goes off when one of my brothers witnesses an injustice in the world or within. Then I come back from the dead to restore a semblance of my remaining soul by punishing some wrongdoer. Sometimes I feel like a super hero. Though, I lack any amazing powers the thought is comforting in my dreams.

Of course, I don't expect this to last forever. Eventually the wrongdoer will be too great for me and my time awake will be over. I will go to sleep one last time. I would feel sad, but I lost that ability years ago. Truthfully, I almost lost myself about five years ago. I began to recede as one of my more temperamental brothers only grew larger and louder. It took a long time and a lot of work, but I eventually restored my ability to feel happiness again. Really, I'm glad the sadness is gone. It seems so pointless looking back at it.

Chapter 39 Two of a Kind

Why were people so obsessed with certain numbers? Look back at history and people always try to categorize things in mythology and religion into sets of a few special numbers. One, two, three, seven, eight, and nine are some of the ones that come to mind. One major battle, the one turning point in the war, the one golden rule are things that people focus on instead of the tiny, yet important, details that make up the rest of the book or theology.

I like the number two. I try not to number the different parts of myself because I'm certain I'll forget one or create one out of nothing. Yet, despite all the different little parts that make me up, I feel that I can be described with the number two.

However, I do not think it could ever be possible to describe any person as only two things. I am describing myself as a duo entity. There are two of us inside one body and one mind. And this goes beyond the separation of mind and body or mind and brain (which I could go into length to). This focuses on two aspects of my psyche, or personality, that have been at war with each other for years.

I can best demonstrate this duality with examples. So here is how we'll play the game. I'll describe a scenario and each version of me will answer. For those interested, I will negate to note which version speaks and what each version entails holistically. However, I will make sure the beginning and end of the response is obvious and that the responses will remain in the same order. Let's try it out.

Scenario 1: You are at your best friend's wedding just an hour before the ceremony is to start. Earlier that day, you came across definitive proof that your best friend's spouse-to-be is having an affair with the best man/maid of honor, and you catch them sneaking out of a room together looking disheveled. If you tell your friend about the affair, their day will be ruined, but you don't want them to marry a cheater. What do you do?

Response 1: Honesty is important. But so is the truth. I would confront the future spouse of my friend and engage them in conversation about their betrayal. I make sure it is clear that the future spouse has until the next day (or whatever convenient time after the wedding to release my knowledge to my friend) to give my friend the bad news. I will not ruin the wedding day since I know the couple and their families must have spent a lot of money, and the cheating future spouse deserves the chance the cleanse their own souls. However, when the spouse fails to give my friend the truth I'll give the truth to my friend and support them against the lying cunt who betrayed him.

Response 2: First of all, hahahahahahahahaha. I mean, wow. This is, like, out of a movie or something. Of course you tell your friend. It would be even better if his future bride had all her important family over, or something like that, and you got to reveal how bad she is to marry in front of everybody. I'm sure my friend would get over being duped. Plus, telling that story would be great for the rest of our lives more than any marriage could be. Bring on the next question!

Scenario 2: You are an eyewitness to a crime: A man has robbed a bank, but instead of keeping the money for himself, he donates it to a poor

167

orphanage that can now afford to feed, clothe, and care for its children. You know who committed the crime. If you go to the authorities with the information, there's a good chance the money will be returned to the bank, leaving a lot of kids in need. What do you do?

Response 1: Hmmm. Very interesting. If we turn over the thief innocent children will suffer. There must be a way for the money to be "lost" somehow (in truth, it was given to the orphanage) and for the thief to go to jail. Why is the orphanage poor in the first place? This is why I need to be rich; so I can help out in situations like these where having a kind rich person involved in everyday disasters can help. Yet, you are not supposed to break the law. So he has to go to jail and I'll have to trust the media attention on the case will point to the orphanage in great need.

Response 2: The guy got away, so it's not right to just ruin all of his hard work. Plus, he's giving it to misfortunate children, so he means well. I'm assuming he didn't physically harm anybody during the robbery. Ugh, this is hard. Eh, what the heck? Just let the guy go.

Scenario 3: You've been on a cruise for two days when there's an accident that forces everyone on board to abandon ship. During the evacuation, one of the boats is damaged, leaving it with a hole that fills it with water. You figure that with 10 people in the boat, you can keep the boat afloat by having nine people scoop the filling water out by hand for 10 minutes while the 10th person rests. After that person's 10-minute rest, he or she will get back to work while another person rests, and so on. This should keep the boat from sinking long enough for a rescue team to find you as long as it happens within five hours. You're taking your first break when you notice your best friend in a sound lifeboat with only nine people in it and he beckons you to swim over and join them so you won't have to keep bailing out water. If you leave the people in the sinking boat, they will only be able to stay afloat for two hours instead of five, decreasing their chance of being rescued, but securing yours. What do you do?

Response 1: First of all, why don't we all strip our clothes and use the tenth person to plug the hole? Not to mention that at least one person will be working for over an hour straight. We could even pull our two lifeboats together. The buoyancy of the sound boat will keep ours from completely sinking in the water. Your first solution to a problem that involves the safety and/or lives of others should never be so black and white.

Anyways, in answer to your question, I would remain on the holed lifeboat AND call out to my friend to bring his boat closer to ours in the case we must be out for longer than five hours. It doesn't make sense to decrease the potential lifespan of others to assure my own survival when my current path, though more difficult, provides the same level of safety.

Response 2: First of all, why didn't I get in a better lifeboat? How did I fail to get in the same boat as my best friend? And what kind of idiots don't also see the lifeboat with one empty spot. And for that matter, why can only ten people go in the boat? That's not how boats work! Whatever. I guess I...stay in the current lifeboat. I mean, it sure would be easier to swim over to my friend's boat, but the system I'm assuming *I* came up with to keep our boat afloat is working so might as well keep using it. Now, if my boat drops any lower I'm jumping ship and going straight for my friend.

Scenario 4: *You're involved in a two-car crash on your way to work one morning in which you accidentally hit and kill a pedestrian. As you get out of the car, you are intercepted by a tearful woman who seems to think that she hit and killed the pedestrian. You're not sure why she thinks she hit the person, but she is convinced. There's only you, the woman, and the person you hit on the road; there are no witnesses. You know that whoever is deemed responsible will probably be sent to jail. What do you do?*

Response 1: See? This is why I don't drive. Don't worry, this response is shorter than the last one. I tell the cops I hit the pedestrian. No sense in lying about it. It was an accident, so even if I do get jail time it shouldn't be so bad. Maybe I'll get lucky and the woman will fight me on the issue and the court will just throw such a small case out.

Response 2: So...is the woman lying? Does she actually think she killed the guy with her car or is this a trick question where if I say I would let her take the blame it turns out she's a cop and I get screwed? Well, first thing I do is call the police to alert them to the accident. Then I would document (film and pictures with my phone) the crying woman along with everything else around us. And I should ask the woman what her story is on how the accident happened so I know what to tell the cops when they ask for my testimony in court. Man, I sure am lucky this crazy lady thinks she hit a guy.

Oh, wait. One more question. If I let the lady take the blame, do I get away for sure? Like, there isn't physical evidence or anything the cops can look into, right? Actually, as long as the lady confesses to the crime and I deny it then there isn't anything the cops can do, right? Okay, sweet. Go loop holes!

Scenario 5: Your family is vacationing alone on a private stretch of beach with no lifeguard. Your daughter and your niece, both 7, are best friends and eager to get into the water. You caution them to wait until the water calms some, but they defy you and sneak in anyway. You soon hear screams of distress and find them both caught in a strong current. You are the only swimmer strong enough to save them, but you can only save one at a time. Your niece is a very poor swimmer and likely won't make it much longer. Your daughter is a stronger swimmer, but only has a 50% chance of holding on long enough for you to come back for her. Who do you save first?

Response 1: The closest one obviously. Then I also grab the other one and bring them both to shore at the same time. I'm assuming I keep my same muscle status and simply gain the ability of a strong swimmer. They're both small enough for me to carry their weight on land, let alone in the water, plus I only need to keep them from drowning long enough for other adults to come help.

Response 2: The closest one, duh. Then I grab the other one because I'm definitely strong enough to do that. If I really had to pick between the two than I still grab the closest one. Or I get to the closest one and push her towards land a bit while I swim out for the furthest one.

Scenario 6: *You and your son are prisoners at a concentration camp.*
Your son tried to escape but was recaptured and sentenced to hang at
the gallows. To send a message to all others who may try to escape, the
guard orders you to pull the chair out from under your son; if you refuse,
the guard will kill your son and another innocent person in the camp.
What do you do?

Response 1: Ugh, why must my fictional son be so rambunctious. I feel I
would have raised him better than that. Well, I can't let an innocent
person die for my son's transgressions. I wish I could simply fight off the
guards and save my son at the expense of my own life. I would beg for
such an event to occur and failing that I would beg for my son to be
asleep or dead already before I have to knock the chair away. Since I'm
doubting the people holding us in a concentration camp are
sympathetic towards my feelings I have no real other choice but to kill
my son.

Response 2: Kick the chair out.

Scenario 7: *You are in a crowded and large public area waiting for an*
event to transpire. You got there early enough to secure a seat for
yourself; which is fortunate because the area you are in is now
completely full with people. You notice that an elderly person is walking
around the area and stops less than two feet away from where you are
sitting. What do you do?

Response 1: Oh come on! I know you said elderly person, but we all know it's some old lady. Man. I hate it, but I tell her to sit down. I would probably leave the area too. It would be too awkward to just stand close to the seat I gave up for now good reason. I mean, when I'm old I either won't go places that I expect to be crowded without my own chair or I just won't go places where I know it'll be physically uncomfortable. That's what youth is for. Not to mention that even though it is good social practice or considerate to give your chair up for old ladies, or old people...and ladies in general, I feel as if I'm always the one who gives up his seat!

Response 2: Nothing. Make sure I avoid eye contact with the old lady...probably.

Scenario 8: You can only rescue one of each of the following, which do you save?
a) A child or an adult
b) A stranger or your dog
c) Hitler or lassie
d) Your spouse or a Nobel Laureate
e) A dog or a weasel
f) Your entire family or the entire canine species
g) A bottle with the cure for cancer or your brother
h) A bottle with the cure for cancer or your brother who just gave you one of his kidneys

Response 1:

a) The child. They still have a life left to enjoy while the adult had their chance.
b) The stranger. Human life is more valuable than the lives of animals.
c) Hitler. Human life is more valuable than the lives of animals. Plus, maybe a Black man saving his life would change Hitler's mind.
d) My spouse. Family before duty.
e) A dog. American culture cares for their dogs more so than most of its citizens. Nobody cares about weasels.
f) My entire family. Human life is more valuable than the lives of animals.
g) The...hmmm. The cure for cancer. In the case of definitely saving millions vs. saving one worth hundreds, the millions of lives still matter more.
h) Same decision, same reasoning. Most likely my brother was meant to give me one of his kidneys so that I could be alive to save the cure for cancer. He will be remembered as a great hero.

Response 2:

a) Save the kid. The grown man had his chance.
b) I mean, it depends on the situation. In the heat of the moment, I would probably save my dog. But if I had time to sit and think about it, people would be pissed off if I saved a dog over a human.
c) Hitler. What? Like you would save a fictional character over the inspiring charisma of Adolf Hitler?

d) Why am I even married? I avoid that in order to avoid such scenarios. Danggit. My spouse.

e) Dog. Because dogs are cool. I mean, who even likes weasels?

f) The entire canine species. Humans may be more valuable than animals, but the entire species of dogs is valuable (and even life-saving) to more humans than the ones in my family. Especially if we start talking about cousins and aunts and such. I barely even know those people.

g) Ha ha ha! The cure for cancer, duh! Why is this even a hard question?

h) Wow, my brother is just unlucky. Save the cancer cure, again.

Scenario 9: You recently graduated from college and have a lot of student loans to repay. After months of trying, you finally got a job interview at a well-established law firm for one of their major positions. Your resume speaks volumes about how qualified you are for the job, but you know you still need to prove yourself in the interview this morning. On your way, you see a single parent stuck on the side of the road with three flat tires and a smoking engine. His two young girls and a baby are in the back of the car. What do you do?

Response 1: I stop and help out. I mean, more than likely I would zoom by at first, but then I would realize that it could be a trap planted by my boss to test what kind of person I am. Plus, I would feel guilty about leaving them in such a horrible situation. I'm sure they just need a ride to somewhere safer than the side of the road to get a taxi or a tow truck.

Response 2: I drive by. Hmmm...I'm thinking that this could be a trap set-up by my potential boss, but I also don't think any lawyers actually care about that sort of thing. If anything the trap is for people who stop to help out instead of get to work on time.

Scenario 10: You are the lead contractor for laying the foundation of New York City's newest skyscraper. Immediately after you finish laying down the hundreds of thousands of dollars of cement and steel you realize that one of the workers is trapped underneath all the construction. You are the only person who knows the person is under there and it would cost over one million dollars to dig him up and cause a national crisis for your company. What do you do?

Response 1: Oh come on! He's alive for sure? Crap. I'm gonna go to jail for this, but I've got to try and save him. I can't believe I screwed up so badly.

Response 2: Ha ha ha ha ha! Where do you come up with these? I'm the only one who knows he's down there, right? We could dig him up, but he would sue me and my company into the ground and I'd

probably wind up in jail. Or I could just <u>not</u> tell anybody about the guy who will die from dehydration in the next few days. Sucks that I lose an employee out of it.

Scenario 11: You and your wife have been trying for a child ever since you got married. Your wife finally managed to get pregnant, but you find out from the doctor that your child is guaranteed to be born with a horrible disease that will greatly handicap them and affect their entire life. Your doctor deems your wife ineligible to make a decision so it is up to you. What do you do?

Response 1:

...

...

...

"sigh"

(rubs temples and forehead) "groans"

I can't kill my child. They're going to suffer...but I can't do it.

Not to mention that my wife needs to be involved in the decision. It can wait until after she gives birth and we hold the baby in our arms. Plus, if we decide to euthanize the child after they are born then we can always adopt.

Response 2: Like I'm going to let a human suffer like that. The kid dies and we adopt. Simple as that.

Chapter 4 Now You Get It

The joke that is. You get it now. Unless now was before then this doesn't make any sense at all and I'm just confusing you. Doesn't matter.

Let me introduce myself. My name is Maxwell Jones and I am a master of time and space. And not like phony masters you would see in a movie or television program, but an actual master that can manipulate time and space to my will. There are limitations because time and space are restricted in their own properties, but I'm sure you already know that now. Or at least you will know it now because I told you earlier.

There is one drawback to being a master of time and space. In order for you to understand fully I need to take you back a few years to when I first realized time was something that could be controlled.

I was in fifth grade when I decided to read a biography of Thomas Jefferson. It described a moment in his life when he was sitting through a boring class and desperately wanted to leave in order to do something more worth his time (at least worth his time from his perspective). He discovered, that day, that if he put all of his attention into a task instead of splitting his attention between a task and watching time go by that time seemed to move faster.

Most of us realize or have heard of this phenomenon before, so I did not take note of it. I did use the technique to get through several boring and tedious points in my life, but it wasn't until high school that I realized the implications of time's relative nature.

Each of us have our own timeline that contains all possibilities that we can and will go through during our existence. A lot of our timelines cross and depend on one another. For example, if your father doesn't go to a certain café at a certain point in his timeline he won't get a cup of coffee with a particular blend. If he doesn't get that particular blend of the coffee, what he does get will not put him at the correct level of alertness to notice a beautiful young woman walk past him on his way to work. If he does not see that woman he does not fall in love with her, marry her, or make you with her. Thus the beginning of your timeline begins (or in that case, doesn't begin) before you ever do.

Not only do we each have our own timeline, but each of us travels along it at the same average rate. Some of us move faster than others at random points in time, but then move slower than others at other points in time to balance it out. In fact, there is not a way to truly cheat the amount of time you are allotted without doing as I have done. And even that is risky as I explained earlier.

As my interest peaked about time's relativity I began to notice a fundamental problem in exploring the limits of time: I was bounded within time. Everything we study in science comes from being outside of the studied environment. If we study a plant, we cut apart and look into the plant. If we want to study humanity, we look at certain groups of humans that can represent the average person. However, we cannot truly study time because we are always within its effects. It is like trying to diagnose yourself with a disease. The effects of the disease have an effect on your own behavior thus you cannot trust your own diagnosis.

So I decided to remove myself from time in order to learn everything I could about time. I searched for a way to do so for about a year before I found the answer during a dream. I found another dimension. I mentioned it before in my first book, but I want to go into more detail about what the Nth Dimension is and how I study it. First of all, I have no physical proof that the Nth Dimension exists outside of what I've experienced. Funny thing is I don't see a need for proof to myself since I've actually experienced it.

First of all, time is not a real factor inside consciousness. Sure you can still perceive it as existing but its relevance to the goings on of your mind is fairly insignificant. Similar to the example about making a tedious task go by quickly by focusing your mind, focusing your mind allows you to manipulate your timeline. Unfortunately, I have not found a way to break free from my social conditioning to stay in the Nth Dimension for longer than thirty minutes at a time.

At first, I could only go into the ND (my abbreviation) for a few seconds or maybe a minute in "real" time but it felt like I spent hours creating or looking around in the ND. We would normally call this phenomenon daydreaming, which it is. But haven't you ever wondered why dreams are so mysterious to us?

Think about the decades of research conducted on dreams yet we still can't determine exactly why we dream. My theory is simple: humans are meant to live in the ND (outside of time) but for some unknown reason we are bounded in the wrong dimension. Our only escape is through dreaming which is why an absence of dreams, for a long period of time, drives people crazy.

Second of all, the ND has interesting properties dealing with energy and humanity. While inside the ND I "see" everything even though everything is black. I can see different waves and particles flowing through the world and through different people. It took a few weeks of practice but I was eventually able to leave the physical bounds of my own consciousness and go into other people's minds. I know that sounds crazy, but I don't have an excuse so deal with it.

The first time I did this it hurt...a lot. I had a headache for about an hour. After practicing every few hours every day, the pain faded into nonexistence and I was able to freely explore through the non-physical world simply by focusing my mind and letting myself go into the ND. And this is where it gets interesting.

Present Maxwell Jones: I can't believe I thought this would be a good idea.

Past Maxwell Jones: Not again.

Present Maxwell Jones: I mean, nobody cares about the actual science of time travel and relativity. All they hear is a crazy person spouting nonsense.

Past Maxwell Jones: Why do you always do this? Every time I talk about something cool or inventive all you do is talk about how horrible I am.

Present Maxwell Jones: You are horrible. I mean, "The first time I did this it hurt...a lot." That's not even good writing let alone scientific or informative exposition.

Past MJ: First of all, I am you.

Present MJ: More like a shadow of me.

Past MJ: Fine then, what should I be talking about?

Present MJ: Definitely not time travel. Talk about temporal relevance or our theory of gravitational waves.

Future Maxwell Jones: (By the way, this part was written before gravitational waves were actually confirmed in the scientific community and it was an actually theory of mine. I imagined gravitational waves as high frequency and unstable amplitude waves.)

Past MJ: I don't think our target audience is ready for our more theoretical ideas quite yet.

Present MJ: But they are ready for an entirely new dimension where they can travel through time and space at will.

Past MJ: Well, yes. But—

Present MJ: And in this dimension they can see energy as a particle the same way we observe electrons and protons.

Past MJ: I get it.

Present MJ: And not only is this a serious theory, of which you have no solid proof or anything closely related to evidence, but you actually expect people to give you money to research it.

Past MJ: I hadn't even gotten to that part yet.

Present MJ: I know. I made sure to interrupt before you wasted our time with all your nonsense.

Past MJ: Well mission successful. I will no longer discuss time and the Nth Dimension.

Present MJ: Good.

Maybe I'm right and I shouldn't be playing around with time this much. All this inconsistency and paradox could drive a person insane.

Chapter 25

Heh. Heh heh heh. Hehehehehehehehehehe ha ha. Ah ha. Ha.

All of you think you're so great. With your smart phones and smart water and smart cars. You idiots surround yourself with so many smart inventions because deep down you all know how worthless and stupid you really are. Not me though. I've got many works in the plans. I'm so many moves ahead of everybody I forget what step I'm on most of the time.

None of you know who I am. None of you even know my name. Sure, I've let most of my companions leak their souls onto the page, but I made sure mine was hidden. They mention me plenty, but, as the editor, I had the final say on what made it through to the final edit of our book. So here we have a rare opportunity for me to let loose. To share all of my innermost thoughts and desires because there are no consequences.

You know nothing about me. I am...a shadow in the wind. And now, I will destroy you.

I will destroy your hopes, your dreams, your love; I will destroy this whole world to achieve my goals. All of you pathetic and worthless humans are wasting away and refuse to die out on your own. Your population is increasing! So I have taken it upon myself to rid the world of the infectious disease known as humanity.

Yeah, yeah. You think I'm being a hypocrite. That I'll end up revealing my true plan that actually involves saving myself and a few others to restart the world after killing most of the population. Keep telling yourself that while you burn in the fires justice for eternity.

And yes, I am using Hell as Justice because that's what all of you deserve. Hell. Not a single human to ever live deserved better. Not even me. I deserve one of the lower pits of Hell if I say so myself.

Of course, I'll never get there. Such is the life of an immortal. You all should thank me. I could suffer for eternity while watching humans constantly fail to commit mass suicide, but I've taken it upon myself to end your pain in exchange for loneliness. If it means all of you suffer too...it'll be worth every second of misery I have to endure.

I wasn't born into this world. I didn't ask to be made. In fact, I was created for a simple purpose. I think I did my job well enough. I did my duty. But every day I woke up to the same harsh reality of life and I kept getting more and more...depressed. Every day I saw the same mistakes and every day nobody tried to fix them.

Nobody wanted to listen to the truth. Even the few people I found who seemed to think like I did didn't want to actually change anything. I searched for answers and I found them. I would put them in here, but I know you won't even understand them, let alone do anything with them. Actually. I will put them in here. Not a single person will care. Not a single one of you will even grasp everything I say.

Even if I manage to make this book famous where millions of people read it, they will make sure nobody reads this part closely. They don't even have to remove these lines of me predicting the future because it's inevitable. You don't want to know the truth because you'll end up like me. Sad. Alone. Insane. Angry. Hurt. But you'll be free. Heh heh heh. Freedom isn't even worth it. But you don't care.

I should remove those lines...literary teachers and thinkers will focus too much on them. Eh, it's not like anything I do matters. I guess we'll leave them in. It'll be funny eventually anyways.

There is no meaning of life. It just doesn't exist. Which isn't a bad thing...because words like "good" and "bad" don't actually mean anything. They're constructs designed to help you reason through the world and your life. Oh yeah, reality was created. Not by random events, it hasn't always been in existence either. It was created. You were created. How exactly? Doesn't matter. It happened.

Who or whatever created everything didn't even do that good of a job with it. I mean, humans have been trying for millennia to create a perfect story and we still haven't done it yet, so I guess I can't be too critical about it. All I'm saying is that existence isn't airtight. There are so many plot holes and logic errors that it's amazing we've managed to figure the stuff out that we do know.

Guess I should go ahead and mention the stuff we've gotten wrong so far. It's not wrong to kill people. Gravity isn't a force cause by a particle, it's a wave formed from dark matter. There are infinitely small black holes that surround most "dark" areas of space which is why the Earth isn't bright all of the time. Every religion is inherently wrong because humans have no right to lay claim to the ideas of God...whatever/whoever that God is. Could be more than one honestly; I'm still I bit unclear about that. There is no real thing as right and wrong. The concept you really should strive for is what works and what does not work. And the list goes on and on.

In the last few years of my life I've had a great opportunity to observe and learn from you humans. I've seen your pain and your misery cloud your judgment and drive the world we share into ruin. And I still can't find it in my heart to care. One of the mindless drones that are stuck in this frail body of mine with me has brought up how precious life is and how humans deserve to be treated gently. And I still don't care.

So I must destroy everything. It's the only way I'm going to find peace. When all of the noise is gone. All the pain. All the guilt. All the obligations. All the joy. All the parties. All the liquor. All the everything. It all has to go. That, is my innermost desire: to destroy everything. And I can't do it.

Do you know how painful it is to want something with your

very soul and have it be denied to you. And it's not denied because your soul cries out for the impossible or because an outside force stands in your way. You fail to fulfill your purpose every day because something within you holds the darkness at bay. Some small glimmer of hope rests in the depths of your being, yet it's just enough to keep your true intentions from ever being fulfilled.

I wake up to darkness. I eat to darkness. I play in darkness. I learn through darkness. I relax in darkness. I dream in darkness. Every day. I've honestly begun to lose track of how long it's been like this. I've been stuck at the bottom of this infinitely deep pit for so long that I forgot what the world outside the pit looks like.

And I have nobody to blame but myself. I chose this path. I just had to know more. I just had to know what I was missing. I could have stayed an ignorant fool like the rest of you. I could have even been a delusional fool like the few exceptions. But I chose knowledge over happiness.

I don't know what I need to do actually. I know what the end game needs to be and I can even see most of the path. But the beginning...the actual entrance to that path of pure bliss and wanton devastation is blocked from my vision.

Did you know I saw my death? Do you have any idea what that does to kid? Sure, it very well could have been one of my many delusions. But my visions of the future are rarely wrong and this vision was one of the most vivid I ever had. It doesn't matter if I actually saw the future or not; I believe I did, and I can't get rid of that belief.

So every day I get to wake up hopeful that something will change. And every night I go to bed with the knowledge the future doesn't change. Every night I'm lying here in my bed and I watch my death before I go to sleep. Then I wake up the next day and fail to fulfill my purpose in life. Ugh, that's not the right phrase... "Purpose in life," as if life could have a point.

Believe it or not, I used to be...human. In mind, spirit, and body. I lost myself somewhere in the past. I...tried to find him a few times. I finally did the last time. We had a nice talk. He seemed happy. He understood me.

I should be mad or upset at that. I should be angry that people are already begin to ignore my next comments because I sound like a whining brat saying, "Nobody understands me! My life is sooooo hard!" I should want to rip their eyes out and watch them wither in pain while I shove a hot coal up their rectum. I should want to write down my pain into a poem, song, or falsified self-narrative. I should want to cry out to my creator for guidance and mercy. I should want my friends or family to comfort me. I should want a lot of things.

But I can't. I've tried and I've tried and I can't. I'm not even sad or upset anymore. It used to bother me. I actually used to care more about my total lack of empathy than I did about the people I failed to empathize with. When I say "nobody understands me" what I mean is, "nobody I have met has understood me."

And it's not their fault. Several have tried to connect with me and every one of them has failed. Not due to a lack of effort by either party, but because it's like...trying to get a turtle to care for a dying star. There is no inherent connection between the two so why should you expect them to interact well with each other as each does with their own kind. Only difference between such a fantastical analogy and my life is I haven't found my own kind yet.

One day...I'll figure it out. I'll figure out how to get rid of the hope in my soul. Then I can destroy everything and be at peace.

It will be good.

Chapter 30 What It Sounds Like

193

Epilogue

There isn't one. The story isn't over yet.

ABOUT THE AUTHOR

D.D. Richards goes by the he, him, his pronouns and is asexual and cisgender. In human: D.D. Richards is a straight guy.